"You know what I mean, Chris. I'm not exactly every man's fantasy."

"In other words, you're not a cross between Betty Crocker and a *Playboy* centerfold."

Allie felt a flash of pain. "Something like that," she agreed, and began walking. The sand was warm against her bare feet.

She got about ten yards down the beach before Chris caught her by the arm and turned her around to face him. "Has it ever occurred to you that you don't know very much about men's fantasies?" he asked, his voice slightly husky. His grip on her flesh became a caress. She caught her breath as his fingers trailed slowly down the length of her arm, finally capturing her hand.

"I never claimed to be an expert on fantasies," she replied.

"And that's a good thing. Because an expert would have realized you've been starring in most of mine . . ."

Other Second Chance at Love books by
Carole Buck

ENCORE #219
INTRUDER'S KISS #246

Carole Buck *is a TV network movie reviewer
and news writer who describes herself as a
"hopeful romantic." She is single and cur-
rently lives in Atlanta. Her interests include
the ballet, Alfred Hitchcock movies, and
cooking. She has traveled a great deal in the
United States, loves the city of London, re-
fuses to learn to drive, and collects frogs.*

Dear Reader:

Signs of spring are popping up all over—what a relief!—and this month's six SECOND CHANCE AT LOVE romances are brimming with all the elements that make radiant love stories. So choose a sunny corner, make yourself comfortable, and enjoy ...

We begin with *Ain't Misbehaving* (#256), another heartwarming read from Jeanne Grant. All-man Mitch Cochran is captivated by gregarious Kay Sanders, but he has a problem. A long-term illness, from which he's fully recovered, kept him bedridden during the years when other young males were struttin' their stuff. Now he's somewhat chagrined to find himself a virgin at 28! To our delight, Jeanne Grant tackles this sensitive subject with tenderness, humor, and masterful skill.

Our next romance, *Promise Me Rainbows* (#257), is by Joan Lancaster, a new writer whose wacky, wonderful story is filled with lovable, eccentric characters. A runaway chimp, two giant St. Bernards, and a mysterious "fairy godmother" keep the action lively, while Alec Knowles's hot-blooded pursuit of feisty Nora Flynn ensures that the romance is offbeat and steamy.

In *Rites of Passion* (#258) by Jacqueline Topaz, Corky Corcoran's life of barely controlled suburban chaos becomes even crazier when she falls head over heels for brilliant, sexy anthropologist Kristoffer Schmidt. This romance has one of the funniest scenes of madcap domestic catastrophe I've ever read. Don't worry, I won't give the surprise away, but I will promise that once you've read *Rites of Passion* you'll never again think of anthropology as a dry-as-dust science!

In *One in a Million* (#259) by Lee Williams, heroine Suzannah isn't rich, but she's having a ball playing the part of a wealthy socialite on her aunt's estate—until her Rolls Royce breaks down in Craig Jordan's humble back yard. Suzannah hires Craig as a gardener and has fun playing a grand lady to his deferential servant. But soon deception piles on deception, and Suzannah becomes determined to exact revenge—with hilariously calamitous results!

In *Heart of Gold* (#260), Liz Grady once again creates a hero you can't help falling in love with. Roarke Hastings, handsome and self-assured, enrolls in Tess Maxwell's dance school to tame his two left feet ... and learns she's a damsel in distress. But are his offers of knightly assistance an expression of true love, or only of heart-felt kindness? Be assured, Liz Grady has written one powerful romance!

Finally, in *At Long Last Love* (#261) Carole Buck presents a funny, moving story of a friendship that blossoms into love. Allie Douglas and her boss, Chris Cooper, have been buddies for years, but something strange is happening to their comfortable companionship. Will it destroy their camaraderie or lead to a more exciting union? Carole Buck's realistic yet thoroughly entertaining approach to her subject makes *At Long Last Love* a special treat.

So, please do get outside and enjoy the fine weather, but don't miss any of this month's SECOND CHANCE AT LOVE romances. And thanks to all of you for sending the hundreds of questionnaires and letters we continue to receive. We love hearing from you!

Warm wishes,

Ellen Edwards

Ellen Edwards, Senior Editor
SECOND CHANCE AT LOVE
The Berkley Publishing Group
200 Madison Avenue
New York, N.Y. 10016

Second Chance at Love

AT LONG LAST LOVE

CAROLE BUCK

**SECOND CHANCE AT LOVE
BOOK**

AT LONG LAST LOVE

First edition published April 1985

First printing

"Second Chance at Love" and the butterfly emblem are trademarks
belonging to Jove Publications, Inc.

Printed in the United States of America

Second Chance at Love books are published by
The Berkley Publishing Group
200 Madison Avenue, New York, NY 10016

Chapter

1

IF POSSESSION OF SEX appeal were a felony, Allie Douglas thought with a mixture of amusement and asperity, Christian Cooper would be at the top of the FBI's Most Wanted list.

It wasn't just his aristocratic good looks—though, heaven knew, the lean, tautly muscled physique, the coin-perfect features, the sable-brown thatch of curly hair, and the remarkable bottle-green eyes certainly helped the cause.

And it wasn't just his astonishing success as one of the hottest commercial directors in the business, either—though his six-figure income and award-winning talents didn't hurt.

No, when all was said and done, Chris simply had enough masculine charm to transform the Hunchback of Notre Dame into a *Cosmopolitan* magazine Bachelor of the Month.

Fortunately, with the lessons of one failed marriage to her credit, Allison Anne Douglas was immune to such things.

Besides, Chris Cooper was her boss—and her buddy. She was his trusted right-hand assistant, and his favorite tennis partner. The only time in their two-year relationship they'd ever kissed had been about eight months before, under a sprig of artificial mistletoe, at the office Christmas party. The less-than-amorous embrace had ended when they'd both opened their eyes in mid-clinch and burst out laughing.

Of course, Allie *had* taken Chris to bed once—in a manner of speaking. It had been about six months after she'd come to work for his company, Strictly Commercial, Inc. Chris had been miserably sick with the flu, and after three days of watching him drag himself around the studio, coughing and sniffling, Allie had hustled him home to his apartment, tucked him into bed, and nursed him back to health.

He'd been a rotten patient: demanding, cranky, and thoroughly unappreciative of her sympathetic efforts to soothe his very fevered brow. To add insult to injury, afterward he'd gone around telling everyone that the only reason he'd gotten well was to avoid having to eat any more of her terrible cooking.

He had, however, been the personification of concern and consideration two weeks later when she'd come down with a similar bug. Predictably, his bedside manner had been nothing short of terrific and, although she'd rather have died than admit it, Allie had been tempted to malinger simply for the pleasure of his *cordon bleu* cuisine.

"Allie!" Chris's commanding voice, crisp and faintly edged with impatience, snapped her out of her reverie. "The damn lights are melting the chocolates again. We need another box."

He didn't even look at her when he gave the order, but Allie didn't mind. She knew his offhand on-the-job treatment of her was an indication of how much he trusted her professionally. Not, unfortunately, that she had been doing very much to merit such trust on this particular day.

Under normal circumstances Chris seldom had to ask her—much less tell her—to do anything. Allie generally anticipated his needs with uncanny accuracy. She might not be able to match Chris's soaring creative talents, but she was a whiz at handling the nit-picking details that could make or break a commercial filming. She and Chris made an excellent working team.

For some reason, however, she'd been less than her usual ultra-efficient self today. Her professional sensitivity to Chris seemed to have been temporarily short-circuited. Oh, she was still extremely— acutely—aware of him and everything he did, but there was a different quality to that awareness . . .

Maybe it had something to do with the lushly romantic, almost erotically-charged atmosphere of this commercial. The tone was supposed to be sexy and adult, and Chris had been unabashedly flirting with the actress doing the ad in order to elicit the mood he required.

The product they were selling was chocolate: "sinfully rich" chocolate, according to the copy, "pure pleasure." The bulk of the commercial—a series of vignettes that had already been shot—was a sensual montage of a darkly handsome man wooing and winning a blondly beautiful young woman with the help of a decadently delicious new brand of chocolate. The final seconds of the commercial, the ones they were trying to get now, involved the woman reclining languidly on a discreetly rumpled, satin-sheeted bed with a dreamy expression on her face and a box of the sponsor's chocolates at her elbow. On cue, she was supposed to pick up a piece, sample it with obvious rapture, and then recite with sultry enthusiasm: "Black Satin—the chocolate that's *not* for children."

Eventually, Allie knew from experience, Chris would get the kind of flawless take he was famous for. He'd also probably end up getting the actress; but then, he was famous for *that* kind of thing, too.

Strange how that thought rankled.

Frowning a little, Allie picked her way deftly across the studio floor to the refrigerator where they had stored about three dozen embossed silver-foil boxes of Black Satin chocolates. She moved with easy, uncalculated grace, her long, thick, toffee-colored ponytail swinging a little with each step. Two years on the job had taught her how to maneuver around the snaking cables and meticulously positioned lighting and camera equipment.

"Thanks," Chris said a minute later as she replaced the box of melting chocolates with a fresh one. He flashed Allie a quick, conspiratorial grin, the fine network of lines at the corners of his eyes crinkling merrily. He flicked her hair with a teasing, careless finger. "What would I do without you?"

"I shudder to imagine," she said, dodging the friendly swat he aimed at her denim-clad derriere. She gave him a brief smile and decided that the curious flush of heat she suddenly felt flooding through her was due to the studio lights.

Suzanne, the actress doing the commercial—privately referred to by the crew as Suzie Space Cadet—tore her adoring pansy-hued gaze away from Chris's handsome profile for a moment.

"Uh—uh..." She had clearly forgotten Allie's name. "Uh, which ones are the orange and strawberry creams again?" she inquired in a breathy little voice. "We *did* decide those flavors go best with my complexion, Coopie, didn't we?"

Coopie? Allie felt like gagging.

"Right, Suzanne," Chris agreed in a velvety tone. He shot Allie a sharp look that warned her she'd be ill-advised to pick up on the nickname. She stared back at him with lambent, brown-eyed innocence for several seconds before assuming a businesslike expression.

"The orange creams are the round ones with the circular design on the top," Allie recited. "The strawberry creams are the dark chocolate rectangles in the corners with the white chocolate squiggles."

Allie knew the chocolate assortment by heart. She'd spent a messy hour dissecting each and every type of Black Satin bonbon in order to determine which fillings were most photogenic. She was thoroughly sick of poking around in mocha praline mousse and framboise-coconut whip. She was also thoroughly sick of Suzanne's repeated inability to remember which were the orange and strawberry creams.

"Max," Chris said, squinting consideringly at Suzanne, "I think the backlighting is a little too hot. We're getting a hint of a halo effect off the hair. Shade it down a fraction."

"Sure thing." The lighting man scrambled to make the delicate adjustment.

Allie returned to the spot where she had been standing, nodding pleasantly to several members of the crew. She glanced around the studio assessingly for several moments, then focused on Chris again. He was back to coaching Suzanne.

"Look, babe," he was saying in an intimate voice.

Even though he had his back to her, Allie knew he was smiling that lady-killer smile of his. "Don't bother with motivation. This isn't the Actors Studio. Say *chocolate* and think sex and we'll be terrific."

Suzanne fluttered her lashes and nodded sweetly. Allie found herself wishing the blonde would bite into a half-frozen piece of chocolate-covered caramel and chip one of her obviously expensive caps. Better yet, she should break out in pimples.

Allie shook her head. What's the matter with me today? she wondered irritably. I'm acting like some kind of . . . of . . . some kind of I don't know what!

Maybe I've got a case of spring fever in August.

Maybe I'm allergic to bubble-brained blondes.

Maybe I should take a vacation from Manhattan and go home to visit Pop in Des Moines.

Allie rocked back on the heels of her sneakers, jamming her hands into the pockets of her jeans. Like the rest of the Strictly Commercial staff, she always dressed for comfort and practicality on shoots; the more elegant items of her wardrobe were reserved for client meetings.

The one whimsical note in her outfit today was the Mickey Mouse T-shirt she had layered underneath the oversized white oxford cloth shirt she was wearing. The shirt was tightly belted and loosely bloused, its volume emphasizing the slimness of her denim-encased hips and long legs.

Feeling oddly uneasy, Allie flipped her ponytail back over her shoulder.

Chris was dressed as casually as the people he employed—with a few telling differences. As he didn't care about status games, the jeans that explicitly molded the muscular leanness of his lower body were well-broken-in Levi's instead of pricey designer denims. He was also wearing a partially unbuttoned short-sleeved shirt made of a vividly colored floral print that would have made a less effortlessly confident man look a bit foolish.

Of course, his feet *were* shod in one-hundred-dollar running shoes, but these were battered and stained with hard usage. And while the timepiece he wore on his wrist *was* a gold Rolex, Allie knew it was an inheritance from his grandfather.

Suddenly, almost as though he felt her eyes on him, Chris glanced across the studio at Allie, his sensuously carved mouth quirking a little as he caught and held her gaze. He shrugged in a smooth but faintly mocking movement, signaling his awareness of the absurdity of what they were doing, then winked at her. A moment later he turned his attention back to Suzanne and the shot he was trying to get.

"Don't drool over the boss, darling," a friendly voice counseled in Allie's ear. "It's very bad form. Amy Vanderbilt would be horrified."

Allie started, her brown eyes widening as she turned to look at Parrish Williams, the free-lance makeup artist who had been hired for this commercial. Standing just a fraction over five-foot-four, he'd had to go up on tiptoe to whisper in her ear.

The product of a decidedly mixed marriage, Parrish blithely described himself as a "racial bouillabaisse." He was outrageously unpredictable, gossipy to the point of being slanderous, and unstintingly loyal to those he considered his friends. Except for his nagging about her failure to fulfill her "style potential"—a complaint usually followed by suggestions that she crop her waist-length brownish-blonde hair, shadow her eyes with a color called neon eggplant, or drape her slim five-foot-eight figure in the creations of some terribly avant-garde Japanese designer—Allie liked Parrish very much.

"I am not drooling over Chris," she denied in a quiet voice. "Why should I?"

Parrish lifted his brows wickedly. "Why shouldn't you, sweetie? Everybody else does."

"I'm not everybody, Parrish," she informed him tartly.

"Thank God for that. But, take it from me, Allie in Wonderland. I know drooling when I see it, and that's what you were doing." He gave her a bright, triumphant smile.

"I was watching Chris coach Suzanne for this next take." Allie fiddled restlessly with the stopwatch she wore suspended from her neck. All right, yes, she supposed she had been staring a little . . . but *drooling?* Never! Chris Cooper wasn't her type any more than she was his. They were friends!

"Of course you were." Parrish's button-black eyes twinkled as he drawled out the words. "But never fear, your secret will be safe with me. My lips are sealed."

"Your skinny neck is going to be strangled with one of your scarves if you don't drop this right now, Parrish," Allie declared in dulcet tones, tugging warningly on the fringed end of the puce silk scarf he had wound around his throat. "Anyway, if you want to talk about drooling, look at Suzanne." She wrinkled her nose in an unconscious grimace of distaste.

Allie had never had any illusions about her looks. She'd always been too tall and tomboyish to be "cute," too strong-featured to be "pretty," and too lacking in feminine and sexual confidence to be "glamorous." At twenty-seven, she'd come to accept her appearance. Her style was practical, neat, and basically wholesome. While she was attractive in a healthy, independent sort of way, Allison Anne Douglas had never been the type to turn men's heads.

Allie's ex-husband had had a lot to do with her unflinching assessment of her lack of appeal. But even if she hadn't come out of her five-year marriage with a pretty battered self-image, she would have had to be both blind and stupid not to grasp the difference between her looks and those of the breathtakingly beautiful women who paraded in and out of the Strictly Commercial studios—to say nothing of in and out of Chris Cooper's personal life.

Allie Douglas was neither blind nor stupid. She had once been very innocent and naïvely trusting, but that was in the past. A lot of things were in the past as far as she was concerned.

"Do I detect a note of disapproval?" Parrish inquired, cocking his head.

"It's not a question of disapproval. But just look at the way she's staring at him. It's like he's some Christmas present she's just dying to unwrap."

"Hmm."

Allie shook her head, surveying Suzanne's flawless beauty. "I know she's gorgeous, Parrish," she muttered out of the corner of her mouth. "But she's so *dense!*"

"Dense, darling? Just because she thinks Angola is where all those cute, fuzzy little sweaters come from?"

Allie rolled her eyes. "Can you imagine trying to carry on a sustained conversation with her?"

"Somehow when you talk about Chris Cooper carrying on with somebody like Suzanne, I don't think in terms of sustained conversations," he remarked.

"You know what I mean."

"Of course I do." He toyed with the fringe on his scarf for a moment, his expression growing thoughtful. "To tell the truth, though, I don't think you have to worry."

"I am not wor—" Allie began to protest in an indignant undertone.

The makeup artist shushed her, holding up a conciliatory hand. "Okay, okay," he murmured. "Take it easy. All I was trying to say is that I think the Clio-winning King of Commercials has been getting noticeably pickier about the women he dates."

"Really? What's his new standard? Their IQs have to be bigger than their bust measurements?"

Parrish feigned shock. "Bitchy, bitchy," he clucked admonishingly. "Seriously, Allie. I've known Chris a lot longer than you have; and take it from me, he's not playing around as much as he used to. In fact, he *never* played around as much as he supposedly used to."

"Oh, come on, Parrish. The contents of his little black book would fill half the volumes in the *Encyclopaedia Brittanica!*"

"Look, I don't contend he's been practicing celibacy. Sure, he's gone through a lot of women, but he's on better terms with ninety-eight percent of his ex-lovers than most guys are with their wives. I've never known him to deliberately hurt somebody. And, to give him credit, he's never gotten involved with anybody who didn't understand the rules of the fast lane."

"I don't think he's ever gotten involved with anybody, *period,*" Allie commented, an odd trace of melancholy shadowing her long-lashed brown eyes.

"Well, you can hardly blame him. His mother wasn't exactly a terrific role model. What's she on now, husband number five? And his father is a cold-fish Philadelphia blueblood. Plus, Chris has had women positively *crawling* all over him since he was fifteen or sixteen..." Parrish gestured expansively. "But, to get back to my original point: I have a sneaking hunch your boss is putting the brakes on his social life. I wish I could figure out why. Maybe he's falling in love."

Allie's heart skipped a beat. "Maybe he's coming down with something," she suggested dryly.

Ten boxes of Black Satin chocolates and two dozen takes later, Chris wrapped the shoot, finally satisfied. Everyone on the crew breathed a sigh of relief. They were all professionals—very skilled professionals, but Chris Cooper was a perfectionist. They knew—from experience—that he was capable of demanding a hundred takes until he got precisely what he wanted.

It was very late in the afternoon by the time everything was completely accounted for. Allie was double-checking the set when Parrish breezed by, makeup gear in tow, firing off a parting suggestion that if she wouldn't cut her hair to a fashionable length, she might at least try a henna rinse or some highlights. She was triple-checking various and sundry odds and ends when the last of the union crew trooped out. And she was about to do a fourth and final check when Chris unceremoniously snatched her clipboard away, announced that he'd booked time for them on the indoor tennis courts at his sports club, and informed her he wasn't about to pay her any more overtime for her obsessive behavior.

"First of all," Allie said, drawing herself up to her full height, "you don't pay me overtime." Since Chris topped six feet by at least an inch, she still had to tilt her head back slightly to look him in the eye.

"Are you sure?" he demanded, a teasing sparkle lighting his green eyes. This was an old routine with them.

"I reconciled my checkbook last weekend, Chris. If I were getting overtime from you, I wouldn't have ended up with a balance of minus seventy-three dollars and twelve cents."

"Are you accusing me of underpaying you, Allie?"

"Second," she continued, "my obsessive behavior,

as you call it, keeps everyone and everything at Strictly Commercial from being swallowed up by your creative chaos!"

"You're not going to throw that fiasco with the pregnant python in my face again, are you?"

Allie smiled sweetly. "Would I do something like that?"

"Absolutely." He nodded emphatically, underscoring his point by tapping the end of her nose. "Look, Allie, I freely admit you've repeatedly saved me from humiliating myself in front of my peers in the Directors' Guild. You're a brilliant producer, Brown Eyes, but you can still be an obsessive compulsive—or a compulsive obsessive—about work sometimes. Now, are we going to get in a few sets or—"

"That's another thing." There was an unusually stubborn set to Allie's jaw and a certain rigidity to her posture. She wasn't sure what was making her feel like this, but she decided to give her emotions free reign. "This is *Friday night,* Chris. Did you ever think of asking me before you went ahead and booked the courts? Did it ever occur to you that I might have other plans?"

There was a short, eloquent silence. She watched a rapid and oddly indecipherable series of expressions flicker over his face as his dark, strongly marked eyebrows came together.

Of course it never occurred to him, you idiot, she scolded herself. You haven't had "plans" on a Friday night since you first met him!

Chris's mouth tightened a little. He had the look of a man forced to confront an unexpected and unpleasant thought. Allie wondered if he was trying to come up with a tactful way of telling her that he'd just assumed someone with her undemanding social schedule would naturally be ready to jump at any and all invitations—no matter how last-minute.

"Look, Allie, I'm sorry," he said slowly, his usual glibness noticeably absent. He ran a hand back through his curly hair in an uncharacteristically awkward gesture. "It's just that you don't usually . . . I mean, I really didn't think—"

"No, you didn't," she agreed, still not sure why she was suddenly making such a fuss. One of the many things she'd come to cherish about her very special friendship with Chris was its easy, stand-on-no-ceremony, play-no-games quality. Yet at this particular moment . . .

Maybe I'm tired of being good old Allie Available, she mused. Maybe I'm tired of Chris taking me for granted as a person . . . as a woman.

She backed away from that last thought almost before it was completely formed. The implications of it shook her more than she was prepared to admit.

Chris was watching her intently, his emerald gaze very steady. He was looking at her as though she were a complete stranger and he was seeing her for the first time. Considering her atypical behavior, she couldn't really blame him for taking such an attitude. Still, there was something disconcerting about it.

"You're right, of course," he said with a nod. "You've got a date with somebody. Who is he? That preppie account exec from the Zeller agency?"

Allie stared at him, momentarily flabbergasted. "Elliot Warner?" she asked in disbelief. "You think he—? For heaven's sake, Chris! The last three client meetings he was at, he looked straight through me." She shook her head.

"The only thing he was looking through was your clothes," Chris returned flatly.

"My clothes? You've got to be kidding!"

"Allie, I've mentally undressed enough women in my life to know the signs. Trust me. Elliot had you wearing nothing but Chanel No. Five."

Allie wasn't certain whether to feel complimented or insulted.

"If you're going out with him, you'd probably better go home and change," Chris went on. "I don't think Mickey Mouse will appeal to a guy who looks like he's been outfitted since birth by Brooks Brothers."

Allie grimaced. How had she gotten herself into this? "I don't have a date with Elliot Warner," she said finally, then added quickly, seeing Chris's brows come together again: "or anybody else."

"Then why...?"

She shrugged. "I don't know. I'm entitled to be moody once in a while, aren't I? I guess I was just reacting to the fact that you *assumed*—"

"Al-lie!" He drew her name out in a gently chiding tone.

"I suppose I wanted to be asked, not just dragged along."

There was a slight pause. Allie had the impression that Chris was making some mental readjustments. She had an unsettlingly mixed reaction to that idea. She didn't want their special relationship to change . . . or did she?

"Would you like to play a few sets of tennis with me tonight?" Chris asked at last. "Assuming—I mean, *if*—you don't have any other plans." He waited a beat then tacked on: "Please?"

Relaxing, Allie gave him a slow, sweet smile. "I'd like that very much."

They played three hard-fought, highly competitive sets. The final score was 6–4, 5–7, 7–5, in Allie's favor. Unlike her ex-husband, Adam Phipps, Chris viewed her athletic abilities with genuine appreciation. At the beginning of their marriage Adam had encouraged Allie's enthusiasm for sports, but he'd grown increasingly critical of it over the years—particularly when it became clear that she was an infinitely better tennis player than he was.

"You've been practicing behind my back," Chris accused her mockingly as they left the club after a quick shower and change of clothes. He draped a casual arm over her shoulders. He still wore his jeans and running shoes, but had substituted a navy short-sleeved pullover for the Hawaiian shirt he'd had on earlier. Allie had traded her work clothes for a peach T-shirt dress cinched to her slender waist with a wide woven belt.

"You were off your usual game tonight," she returned modestly, aware of the intimate brush of his thigh against hers.

"Off, hell. I had my eye on your legs instead of the ball. Those little white shorts you were just barely wearing constitute unsportsmanlike behavior as far as I'm concerned."

"Excuses, excuses." Allie laughed, ignoring the frisson of pleasure that danced up her spine. She was not about to tell him that she, too, had been unusually conscious of his legs—of his whole body!—during their match.

"You've got gorgeous gams, sweetheart," he told her, doing a passable imitation of Humphrey Bogart.

"Thanks."

They walked a block and a half in silence, their steps unthinkingly in synch.

"You want an ice-cream cone?" Chris asked, nodding toward the brightly colored "dessert boutique" that beckoned on the corner up ahead.

"Hmm..." The sound was neutral.

"God, please don't tell me you've started counting

calories, too." Chris had a passion for good food and was a superb cook. He frequently complained that Allie was the only woman he knew who wasn't perpetually on a diet.

"If I don't watch my figure, no one else will," she retorted flippantly.

He stopped and turned to look at her. "Just what is that supposed to mean?" he demanded.

"Mean?" she echoed, taken aback by his abrupt change of mood. There was an unnerving jut to his jaw. "It's just an expression, Chris." Her wide-set brown eyes were puzzled as she gazed up at him.

"Have you got something going I don't know about?" he asked in a lighter tone, his facial muscles relaxing slightly. "You might as well tell me if you do, you know. I'm bound to hear the details from Parrish sooner or later."

Allie pulled a face. "There are no details to tell."

"Then what's with you?"

"Nothing's with me," she responded a trace defensively. Who did he think he was, cross-examining her like this? She'd had enough of that, growing up as the only sister of three fond and often stubbornly protective older brothers.

"Well, you haven't been yourself lately." He sounded half concerned, half irritated. "Do you have a problem, Allie? You know I'll do anything to help if you do."

She looked away for a moment. "No. Everything's just fine." She hoped the declaration sounded more convincing to his ears than it did to hers. She cleared her throat. "But what about you? Manhattan's biggest gossip thinks you're going through a mid-life crisis or something."

"Parrish thinks I'm having a mid-life crisis? I'm thirty-four, for crying out loud. Give me a break!"

"He says your social life is slowing down."

"Well, I—"

"He thinks you're falling in love."

Chris's features went stony, completely devoid of expression. "No way," he declared flatly. "It will never happen."

There was silence for the space of several heartbeats as pedestrians jostled by them unnoticed. Biting the inside of her lip, Allie wished she'd never mentioned Parrish's stupid speculation.

"Chris," she began tentatively, wanting to apologize . . . or *something*. The signals passing between them were so confused tonight!

"It's okay, never mind," he said, brushing the matter away with a dismissive gesture of one hand. His face cleared. "So, to get back to the important question. Do you want an ice-cream cone?" His tone was offhand.

Allie sighed, giving herself a mental shake. Okay. Things were returning to normal. "No, thanks, I don't think so," she decided.

"How about a weekend in the Hamptons?" The inquiry was as nonchalant as the previous one.

"Excuse me?"

"A weekend at my new beach house," he elaborated.

"Ah . . ." What is going on here? she asked herself.

"If you don't have any plans for tomorrow and Sunday, how about coming out with me?" His expression was bland, but she heard the teasing emphasis on the word *plans*. "You haven't seen the place yet. And the weather's supposed to be perfect."

Allie considered for a few moments. Two days of sun and sand sounded tempting, but she wasn't in the mood for the Hamptons style of summer socializing.

"No parties," Chris added, accurately discerning the reason for her hesitation. "We can lounge around, swim a little, and maybe go over a few details on that perfume thing we'll be shooting on Antigua in two weeks. I'll even do all the cooking."

Allie's eyes sparkled. "You talked me into it."

He chuckled. "You are so predictable. Okay. I'll pick you up about eight tomorrow morning." They started moving again. Chris glanced around. The sports club was within walking distance of the refurbished SoHo loft where he lived, but it was more than a hundred city blocks from Allie's Upper West Side apartment near Columbia University. They were headed vaguely in the direction of a subway entrance. "Let's stick you in a cab," Chris said unexpectedly.

"A cab!" Allie protested, shaking her head. Her long, thick ponytail moved back and forth.

"Yeah, it's late," he told her, signaling an approaching yellow taxi with a commanding wave. "I don't like the idea of you riding home alone on the subway so late at night. Especially not on a Friday."

Allie didn't quite know how to react to this sudden show of solicitude. "Chris," she said reasonably, "in case it's slipped your mind, I've been getting around on a subway by myself just fine for the past two years. I'm almost twenty-eight years old. I'm a big girl."

His compelling green eyes flickered over her. "Maybe that's what I'm worried about," he muttered as the cab screeched to a halt in front of them. He pulled the car door open with a jerk.

Allie clicked her tongue. You were the one who was tired of being taken for granted, she reminded herself.

"One of you gonna get in or what?" the cabbie asked grouchily.

"Humor me, Brown Eyes."

Allie shrugged good-naturedly. "Don't I always?"

Chapter

2

"I'M GOING TO get you for this, Chris," Allie declared for the fifth or sixth time late Saturday afternoon. She was sitting on the newspaper-covered floor of one of the bedrooms in Chris's new beach house, stirring a freshly opened can of ivory-toned wall paint with more vigor than was strictly necessary. "I am definitely going to get you." She wrinkled her nose, trying to fight down the urge to scratch the tip of it. Her hands were filthy, and she had no desire to get any more paint on her face than was already there.

"So you keep saying," Chris returned from his perch midway up an aluminum stepladder. He dabbed judiciously at the last unpainted stretch of molding that ran around the top of the wall. He was wearing nothing but ancient khaki-colored shorts and a pair of grungy sneakers. His dark curly hair was attractively disheveled. A subtle ripple of muscle played along his tanned back as he reached with the paintbrush.

Allie gave up trying to ignore the itch on her nose. What did a few more splotches matter, anyway? She got to her feet in a smooth movement, wiping her palms on the faded extra-large 82nd Airborne T-shirt she had on over a pair of skimpy denim cutoffs. The T-shirt had been a present from her next-to-oldest brother, Mark, who was an Army major.

"You are such a con artist," she complained, tossing her braid over her shoulder in an impatient gesture. She'd plaited her hair back in hopes of keeping it reasonably clean, but the scheme hadn't worked very well. The entire toffee-colored length was spattered with paint. She'd probably have to shampoo it with turpentine!

"Con artist?" Chris challenged, glancing over his shoulder with brows lifted in a faintly offended expression.

"Con artist!" she confirmed. "When you invited me out here yesterday, you said something about lounging around, swimming, and home cooking."

"I fed you two hours ago." His mobile, well-shaped mouth twitched with amusement.

"Sandwiches and beer from a deli don't count. Especially not when *I* had to pay for them!"

"Just wait until dinner, Allie."

"I may be dead of exhaustion by then." She stretched up on her toes, easing the tension from the muscles in the small of her back. She hadn't worn a bra underneath the T-shirt, and despite the roominess of the garment, the movement of her small, firmly rounded breasts was evident. "Tell me: do all your guests get stuck painting walls, regrouting bathroom tiles, and washing windows?" she inquired.

"Only the ones I really like," he told her with a flashing grin. The smile did not reach his slightly narrowed eyes.

"Gee, thanks." She picked up a clean brush and dipped it into the can of paint. She was aware of Chris's gaze on her and experienced a fleeting sense of regret at her bedraggled state. "I suppose the ones you don't like have to settle for a weekend sunning themselves on the beach and lapping up white-wine spritzers."

In truth, her grousing was mainly for effect, and she knew Chris was aware of it. Allie certainly didn't object to hard work, and she enjoyed fixing things up. There had been no male-female division of labor in the motherless Douglas household when Allie was growing up. Her father, John, who had been widowed by a car accident just months after Allie's birth, had seen to it that chores were shared. It hadn't been unusual for her oldest brother, J.J., to be baking a pie in the house while Allie was outside battling crabgrass or learning to repair the family car. Her youngest brother, Rick, had liked to say that she was kept from the kitchen by order of the Public Health Department.

Adam had pointed out her failures as a homemaker, too, but the humor in his criticisms had gone sour very quickly. Her ex-husband wasn't precisely a chauvinist, but he'd made it clear before their break-up that while he hadn't minded her having a career, he had expected her to devote herself primarily to the "wifely"—that is *womanly*—duties of marriage.

Allie frowned at the thought of her own inadequacies and wiped the dripping brush on the edge of the can in an automatic gesture.

"Allie?" Chris asked. "Are you okay?"

She blinked. "Oh, sure, I'm fine."

"We can quit now if you want," he offered.

"Don't be ridiculous."

"Well, I don't want you to think you have to—"

"It's all right, Chris."

There was a fractional pause. Glancing at him, Allie saw the same strangely assessing look on his face she had glimpsed the day before. What is he thinking? she wondered.

"You're the first person I've had out here, you know," he said suddenly, his voice quiet.

She gave him an impish smile. "I'm overcome with gratitude."

Shaking his head a little, he came down off the ladder. "You should be, Brown Eyes." He laughed. "I can name about two dozen women who'd love to be here."

"I'll bet," she scoffed. "I can just see Suzie Space Cadet ruining her manicure sanding down the front porch."

"Suzie Space—who?"

"Why, *Coopie,* don't tell me you've forgotten?" Allie fluttered her lashes in an outrageous parody, her voice going breathy, and sugar-sweet.

The imitation—to say nothing of the nickname— registered immediately.

"Allie . . ." he said warningly, advancing on her.

She danced back a step. "'Say *chocolate* and think sex,'" she quoted mockingly.

"You know, when you act like this, I'm amazed your brothers let you live past the age of eight."

"J.J., Mark, and Rick didn't have any choice. Pop said it was unsportsmanlike for them to beat up on me because I was smaller than they were." Her father had been a high-school athletics director in Des Moines before his retirement, and sportsmanship was a key virtue in his eyes. "Besides, I learned how to fight dirty."

"Oh, yeah?"

"Yeah!"

Allie had only meant to daub him with a bit of paint, but she got a little carried away as she swiped at his body with the brush. When she realized what she'd done, she dropped the tool with a thud.

"Why you little—!" Chris exclaimed, looking down at the streak of ivory paint that now ran from his collarbone, down through the springy mat of his chest hair, to the low-riding waistband of his ragged shorts.

"It—it looks like a r-racing stripe!" Allie sputtered irrepressibly, then let out a shriek as Chris made a grab for her. Nimble as a deer, she whirled and raced from the room.

She actually got outside the house and a few yards away before Chris caught her. He tackled her on the gently downward incline of a sand dune, and momentum caused them to roll over together several times. Despite her struggles, Allie ended up flat on her back with Chris straddling her hips and holding her firmly captive. He trapped her wrists deftly and pinned them above her head with one hand.

The rubber band that had been holding her braid had snapped, and most of her hair had come loose. With his free hand, Chris carefully brushed the wayward blond-brown strands off her face, his fingers trailing over the smooth, sun-tinted skin of her cheeks.

"Too bad for you I don't have any scruples about beating up on someone smaller than I am," he observed, gazing down at her with a decidedly smug expression.

"Let me go," she cried. As she tried to squirm out of his grip, a part of her was shockingly aware of the warmth and thrust of the lower portion of his body. Although he wasn't hurting her in the least, there could be no doubt of his physical dominance over her at this moment. And that domination aroused some very disturbing emotions inside her. Allie squirmed again, giving a small grunt of frustration.

Chris wasn't even breathing hard. His naked, paint-smeared chest rose and fell steadily. "A racing stripe, huh?" he demanded. "I suppose I'm lucky you didn't decide to put the Mark of Zorro on my bu—"

"Chris!" Her voice went up. Green eyes met brown.

"Don't pretend to be shocked, Allie. As the mastermind of the only successful BVD raid on a men's dorm in your alma mater's history, you can't claim to be—"

"You promised you'd never repeat that story after I told it to you!" Allie protested heatedly. "Will you let me *up!*"

He shook his head coolly, surveying his body with a grimace. "God, this stuff is all over me," he commented.

"Well, maybe you'll have to shave your chest!" She tried to arch her back. "Come on, Chris, let me go."

"Not until I'm good and ready. This is one of the few times I've ever felt in complete control of you, and I'm enjoying the sensation."

"The illusion of power, don't you mean?" Allie retorted. She was beginning to sound a bit breathless.

Chris shifted slightly, leaning over her, and Allie was conscious of the masculine tang of his perspiration and the faintly spicy scent of his after shave.

"Look, do you want me to cry *Uncle?*" she asked, striving for a light note and missing by a wide margin. Her heart was beating out a strange rhythm.

The sculpted features of the man looming over her seemed both completely unknown and totally familiar. Allie blinked once, twice, desperately telling herself it was only a trick of the sun that was making Chris's face—the same face she'd been looking at for two years—so suddenly . . . devastatingly . . . attractive to her.

"I don't want you to cry anything," Chris told her solemnly.

Whatever she was feeling, he was apparently feeling it, too. Despite the glow of the late afternoon sun, his pupils had dilated wide and dark. There was a faint flush along the strong line of his high cheekbones, and she could see the pulsing of a small vein in his right temple. The wind ruffled his already disordered hair with invisible fingers.

Overhead, a bird called out stridently. Chris's lean body went taut.

"Chris . . ." she got out, trying not to tremble. Her lips parted slightly. She didn't know which would be worse: to have him make a pass—or to have him pull back.

"I got paint on you," he remarked in an absorbed tone, tracing a feather-light path down her torso. Some of the paint from his chest had rubbed off on her T-shirt. The touch of his forefinger burned through the cotton fabric. She could feel her nipples harden in response.

Allie bit the soft inner flesh of her lip, torn by both the desire to surrender and the need to resist. This kind of thing would never work between the two of them! She wasn't Chris's type: anyone in his or her right mind could see that. And even if Allie did understand "the rules of the fast lane," as Parrish had put it, she realized she was incapable of living by them.

Besides, she thought painfully, if you weren't woman enough for Adam, how could you ever hope to satisfy Christian Cooper—even on a very temporary basis? And you know temporary relationships are the only kind Chris has.

She swallowed. "Chris, let me up, please."

His eyes were fixed on her mouth as though he were committing the soft, rosy contours to memory. Her lips felt dry, and she had to restrain the natural instinct to moisten them with her tongue. Despite herself, she couldn't help wondering what it would be like to have Chris kiss her for real, just once . . .

"Please," she repeated, a little more firmly this time. This was crazy! She and Chris loved each other as friends and respected each other as colleagues. To risk the close relationship they had built up over the past two years because of some fluky physical attraction was insane!

Chris took a deep breath and let it out very slowly. He then released her wrists and swung his body off hers. Regaining his feet in a lithe movement, he extended a hand to help her up. After a fleeting hesitation—a hesitation she knew he saw and correctly interpreted—Allie accepted his assistance.

"I—I'm sorry about that," she said awkwardly, nodding at his chest. She averted her eyes for a moment, trying to compose herself. A breeze sent her loosened hair billowing across her face like waves of honey-toned silk, and she brushed the errant tresses back behind her ears with an impatient gesture. She cleared her throat. "Really, I didn't mean to—to get paint all over you."

Chris shrugged. Except for a hint of stiffness in his usually easy posture, his manner was back to normal.

Allie felt a stab of resentment at his ability to appear so casual. Well, what did you expect? she asked herself acidly. Whatever you experienced a few minutes ago, it was just a passing fancy for him—an itch.

"There's no problem," Chris told her. "I'm washable. I suppose I deserved something for luring you here with promises of leisure and then exploiting you as an unpaid handyman—handywoman?" He exaggerated his look of polite inquiry.

Allie picked up the cue. "Handyperson," she said definitely, giving a little nod.

"Anything you say." He ran a hand through his hair. "Why don't we quit for the day?" he suggested. "You can take a shower while I start dinner."

"Okay." She forced herself to relax.

"Okay." He underscored the word a little with his voice. He smiled at her suddenly, his expression endearingly apologetic and ruefully tender for a moment. Then he raised one dark brow teasingly.

"What?" she asked, her own lips curving upward.

"You really meant it when you said you know how to fight dirty, didn't you?" he returned. "You look like that character, Pigpen, in the Peanuts comic strip."

She pulled a face. "Thanks, Chris. You certainly know how to make a woman feel good." She began brushing herself free of sand.

"I try, Allie."

Chris and Allie spent a pleasant, peaceful evening together. They ate outside on the open porch of the beach house, dining on barbecued steaks, foil-wrapped potatoes cooked in the coals of the grill, a huge fresh salad, and a bottle of Beaujolais. Afterward, they engaged in a cutthroat game of Monopoly, which ended when Allie was plunged into bankruptcy by a series of unlucky throws of the dice.

They both tried to behave as though nothing unusual had happened between them earlier in the day and, for the most part, they succeeded in recapturing their easy, buddy-buddy relationship. It was only late in the night, as Allie tossed and turned on the sofabed that was one of the few pieces of furniture in the house, that she found herself wondering what was going on—

and why. She took no comfort from the fact that Chris, bedded down next door in a sleeping bag, was apparently enjoying a deep, trouble-free slumber.

They worked on the house again Sunday morning. The place was fairly small and relatively isolated. It was just right for the kind of retreat Chris was planning. The weathered-wood exterior exuded a battered charm that blended perfectly with the sandy, sparsely vegetated surroundings. Although the interior would never qualify for a feature in *Architectural Digest*, Allie instinctively knew it could be transformed into a comfortable refuge.

The lure of the water proved irresistible in the afternoon. They swam and frolicked for about an hour before sprawling out on the beach to enjoy the sun. The tension between them seemed to dissolve in the enchanting warmth of the day. Allie accepted Chris's offer to spread tanning lotion on her back without a qualm, relishing the sleek stroke of his palms on her bare skin with innocent pleasure. She then returned the favor, firmly ignoring her strangely heightened awareness of the strength and width of his shoulders and the smoothly muscled power of his torso. His skin felt like heated silk beneath her fingers.

It was only as dusk began to fall that their free-and-easy mood altered. They were lounging on the porch, drinking freshly brewed iced tea spiked with fragrant sprigs of mint, and clearly putting off the start of their trip back to Manhattan.

Allie was sitting sideways in a canvas-and-wooden chair, her legs draped casually over the arm. She was wearing white cotton-duck shorts and a stretchy turquoise-and-white striped top. Her long hair, smelling faintly of herbal shampoo, was pulled back from her face by white combs. She sipped at her drink absently, surveying the horizon without really registering the view.

Chris was on the floor, leaning back against the leg of her chair, his head tilted within reach of her fingers. He had on jeans and a partially unbuttoned work shirt. His eyes were half hidden by his lids and there was a twist to his mouth.

Allie sighed to herself, taking another swallow of the iced tea. She swirled a strand of hair around one finger.

Chris set his glass down with a clink. "Do you think about him much?" he asked suddenly.

"Him who?"

"Your ex-husband. Alfred."

"Adam," Allie corrected automatically. Chris had some kind of fetish about calling her ex-husband by every name but the correct one.

"Adam and Allie. It sounds like a TV sit-com."

"We had some good—great—times," Allie said, wondering what had prompted this unexpected line of questioning, and where it was leading. "But it wasn't all laughs."

"You *do* think about him." He had shifted his body so that he could look up at her, his eyes very steady as they searched her face.

Her soft mouth tightened. "Chris, we were married for five years! Of course I think about him." She did not add that in recent months her main thoughts about Adam had involved comparing him—less than favorably—to Chris.

"The break-up really hurt you." It was not a question. "I remember the day you showed up at Strictly Commercial to apply for the assistant's job. God, you were about fifteen pounds underweight and those big brown eyes of yours—"

"Look," Allie broke in, "I was the first person in the history of my family to get divorced! My husband had left me for a sweet, petite blonde who probably came equipped with the *Good Housekeeping* Seal of

Approval. I felt like a total, utter failure."

"And now?"

"And now, what?"

"Do you still feel like a failure?"

Allie hesitated, rattling the ice in her glass. "I'll always feel like a failure, in a way, as far as Adam is concerned," she said quietly. "He was my husband. I wanted to please him, to make him happy. But I couldn't."

She and Adam had met when they were both in college. He'd been her first and only lover—the first and only man she'd ever dated seriously, in fact. Largely because of the way she'd been brought up, Allie had always been too busy being "one of the boys" to think about trying to attract any of them.

They'd married during their final year at school and moved to Chicago after graduation. Adam had taken a job in the advertising department of a large corporation, and Allie had found a position as a gofer in a film-and-television production house.

They'd had two very good years. Adam did extremely well, while Allie moved rapidly up the ladder in terms of responsibility, if not salary. Then things began to change: subtly at first, then more and more dramatically.

Adam's company was a conservative one that placed a premium on socializing. Allie wasn't particularly good at cocktail chitchat and dinner-party diversions. Adam began dropping hints about—then flatly criticizing—her breezy, informal style and her inability to pass muster as a corporate wife. He also started openly begrudging the time she was spending on her job, especially since she was earning what he considered a very paltry salary for her efforts.

While Allie never neglected the housework, it had always been plain that she preferred eating to cooking and that she wasn't about to devote her energies to attaining the rigid standards set by Adam's mother. Adam found fault with that as well.

Toward the end of their marriage he began finding fault with Allie sexually, too. With no previous experience of men to rely on, no innate wellspring of feminine confidence to buoy her up, Allie took his accusations to heart. The final, scarring blow had come when he'd told her there was someone else, someone who could give him "what a man needs." He hadn't had to spell out what he meant by that cutting phrase.

Adam Phipps didn't destroy Allie's faith in herself as a person, but he did shatter her fragile confidence as a woman. She'd emerged from the divorce deeply hurt and grimly determined never to repeat the mistake of trying to be something she wasn't.

Unwilling to remain in Chicago after the break-up and too proudly independent to go back to her family, Allie had moved to New York City. She'd stumbled into the job at Strictly Commercial almost by chance, following up on the suggestion of an acquaintance of a client in Chicago who'd been impressed by her work.

"Did he make you happy, Allie?" Chris broke into her thoughts.

Allie closed her eyes for a moment, unaware of the vulnerability of her expression. "Chris, I really don't want to talk about this."

"You've talked about it before." That was true. Over the course of the past two years they'd exchanged quite a few confidences.

She looked at him. "Well, I don't want to talk about it now," she said firmly.

She had the impression he was reading a great deal into her refusal to continue with the discussion. "I'm sorry," he returned after a moment. "I didn't realize

I'd hit such a sensitive nerve."

"It's not that," she began, gesturing helplessly. "Oh, I don't know what it is!"

"It hurts to talk about . . . Adam," he said quietly, pronouncing her ex-husband's name very carefully. "I can understand that. You fall in love, commit yourself to someone, get married—"

"Have you ever considered getting married, or committing yourself to someone?" Allie blurted the question out. A split-second later, seeing his face cloud, she wished she could recall it.

There was a long silence. "What do you think, given my track record?" Chris returned finally, an acid hint of mockery edging the inquiry.

A tiny line appeared between Allie's fair brows. He'd sidestepped the question. "Parrish says you're on better terms with your ex-lovers than most men are with their wives," she commented lightly.

"Now that's what I call a glowing endorsement." She could see the working of a muscle in his jaw as he looked away from her and out toward the beach. "Having a long-term relationship with a woman has never really been a priority with me," he said slowly. "Hell, I suppose I could take the Freudian way out and blame my mother. There was a big, messy scandal when she dumped my father, you know, and I guess that soured me on the sanctity of marriage. To say nothing of the cumulative impact of her subsequent trips to the altar. I can understand her not being satisfied with one man. What gets me, though, is her apparently compulsive need to marry every man she sleeps with."

"Your father never remarried, did he?" Allie knew that Chris's father had won custody of him in a very public, very nasty court case following the divorce. She also knew, from Chris's occasional reminiscences about his youth, that Parrish's description of Browning Christian Cooper as a "cold-fish Philadelphia blueblood" was probably an understatement.

Chris shook his head. "He did keep mistresses, though."

"You never told me that!" Allie was genuinely surprised by the revelation. She swung her long legs off the arm of the chair. "Chris—"

He faced her again, holding up one hand. "Allie, there's just no easy way to work that kind of thing into a conversation."

"But—"

"And before you protest that you've told me all the Douglas family secrets dating back to the year one, let me remind you that your skeletons in the closet are strictly of the all-American wholesome variety. As far as I can figure out—and believe me, Brown Eyes, I envy you for it—your childhood was one continuous episode of *My Three Sons* plus one."

She couldn't argue with that.

"Of course, my father was very discreet about his indiscretions," Chris went on offhandedly. "It wasn't as sordid as it sounds."

"I think it sounds sad," Allie said bluntly. She was thinking about more than his father's mistresses.

He shrugged, brushing the shin of one of her legs lightly with his knuckles. "Not so sad. I lost my virginity—to say nothing of my innocence—to one of my father's lady friends." He paused. "They say a boy always remembers his first woman. Well, Judith certainly was memorable."

Allie swallowed, trying to get a fix on his tone. Chris had jokingly alluded to something like this once or twice in the past, but she had never quite taken him seriously. Now, though...

"Were you in love with her?" she asked.

He gave a humorless laugh. "I was sixteen and she seduced me. What are you imagining, Allie? That I've been carrying a torch for some older woman all these years?"

"No, of course not," she answered quickly. "I was just wondering, that's all."

"That's *all* you were wondering?"

"Never mind."

"Have you ever wondered why I've never made a pass at you?" he asked without warning.

If the ground had suddenly opened up and swallowed her, Allie wouldn't have been more surprised.

"No!" she managed to get out in appalled denial, feeling as though she might choke on the single mendacious syllable. That Chris could ask such a question after what had been going on between them...

"This isn't a proposition," he said evenly, catching and holding her gaze, "but haven't you ever thought about us having an affair?"

Allie's normally glib tongue seemed to be stuck to the roof of her mouth. She cleared her throat. You are a twenty-seven-year-old divorcée, she told herself fiercely, not some virginal teenager! This isn't a come-on from a stranger in a singles bar.

"Well, we've known each other for two years, Chris," she temporized. "I suppose..." She shifted uncomfortably.

"Have you?" he pressed, his green eyes boring into her brown ones.

She took a deep breath. She couldn't lie to him—or to herself. For better or worse, a friend had asked her a direct question. For better or worse, she was going to give him a direct answer.

"You're very... attractive... Chris. And lately— look, I'd have to be completely abnormal not to have thought about going to bed with you. And I don't think I'm that abnormal." The wry bravado in the last sentence couldn't quite cover up the deep-seated insecurity that prompted the words. "At least not completely."

He nodded once, an expression she couldn't identify flickering in the depths of his eyes. Allie couldn't decipher his reaction to her words. It was as though she had suddenly lost her ability to comprehend him, as though she had picked up a familiar book in English only to discover it had been translated into some totally unknown language.

She gnawed at her lower lip for a moment as he sprang lightly to his feet and went to stand by the porch railing. A slight tension in his posture and the quick clenching and unclenching of one fist revealed an inner turmoil.

"Have *you* ever thought about us having an affair?" she asked at last. "I mean, you and me going to—"

"I know what you mean," he cut her off abruptly. There was a taut silence. "Not exactly."

Not exactly?! Allie felt relieved . . . disappointed . . . insulted . . . and totally confused—all in the space of less than a second.

He looked at her. "Allie, you're my friend—"

"But I'm not your type?" she interrupted. Hadn't she been telling herself that?

"No!" It came out sharply. Allie didn't know whether Chris was denying her comment or underscoring it. But it didn't really matter. She knew what he was trying to say.

"I'm just one of the guys, right?" she prompted helpfully. She didn't mind the designation. Heaven knew how many men had told her that. And nearly all of them had meant it in the nicest, most admiring way possible.

"You're something special to me, Allie. You—"

"I know. I'm like the kid sister you never had." That was another line she'd heard over and over.

"Dammit, Allie, will you stop trying to stuff words in my mouth!" he exploded, slamming his fist against the railing.

Allie's eyes opened wide as she stared at him. She realized she was trembling a little. Chris yelled around the studio a lot—especially at her—but she had never, ever heard him sound so furious before. She'd also never seen him so visibly angry.

"I—I'm sorry," she faltered. Oh, God, what was going on? Why was everything suddenly going so wrong?

Chris took a deep steadying breath. He jammed his hands into the pockets of his jeans, then took them out again. He crossed his arms over his chest and shook his head.

"No, I'm the one who's sorry," he said wearily. "You were moody Friday. I'm moody today. We were both . . . moody . . . yesterday."

Moody. It was a safe enough word; it covered a lot of possibilities without getting down to specifics— or reasons.

"Maybe I *am* going through a mid-life crisis," he commented, more to himself than to her.

"At age thirty-four?" she asked, in a parody of their earlier conversation.

"Yeah." He laughed, although the sound had a certain whistling-in-the-dark quality to it. He uncrossed his arms and walked back over to her. "I apologize for blowing up at you," he said, brushing his fingertips very gently down the line of her cheek. It was the kind of casual contact she was used to from him, but there was nothing casual about the melting, quivering feeling it evoked in her. Allie fought to keep her face expressionless.

"That's okay," she told him. "I—I understand."

He gave her a crooked smile. "I hope you do." He hesitated for a moment as though searching for the right words. At last he said, "Look, Allie, having a woman—women—to go to bed with has never been any problem for me. But having a woman I could trust, as a friend..." He shrugged helplessly. "There are plenty of Suzie Space Cadets around, but there's only one Allison Anne Douglas."

Allie's eyes were a little too bright as she smiled back at him. "You don't know what you'd do without her, huh?" she asked, getting up out of the chair. There were only a few inches between them and she could feel the warmth of his body.

He stopped smiling. "I shudder to imagine."

The next two weeks sped by, comparatively trouble-free by the ulcer-inducing standards of the chaotic world of commercial-making. Allie managed to shove most of the more disconcerting implications of her weekend with Chris out of her mind. He, as far as she could tell, had done the same thing.

And yet there were moments when she'd sense him looking at her, although she never precisely caught him at it. She could feel his gaze, curious, assessing, perhaps even a little angry, touch her from time to time. It disturbed her, and she had the feeling it disturbed Chris as well.

There were moments, too, when *she'd* watch *him*. Covertly. Almost unwillingly. She was conscious of the virile, masculine strength of his body, of his elegantly disciplined movements. The most familiar things about him—his easy charm, his free-wheeling intelligence, the passion he poured into his work—suddenly seemed fresh and fascinating. And it was during those moments that the thoughts Allie was trying to shove out of her mind shoved back.

The "highlight" of the period prior to their location shoot in Antigua was the auditions for a series of commercials for a new line of snack foods. The campaign stressed the claim that the snacks were highly nutritious as well as good-tasting, and the ads were to feature healthy-looking youngsters engaged in various sports activities. Moreover, the client had specified that the child models had to be "real" and "fresh"—for which those directly involved in the casting silently groaned while mentally substituting the words *inexperienced* and *untrained*.

Personally, Allie adored kids; but professionally, she approached child performers with a great deal of wariness. Some children, of course, were wonderfully natural and a delight to work with. Others, however, were miniature prima donnas, many of them frighteningly, heartbreakingly old beyond their years.

Allie often wondered how a six-or seven-year-old child coped with the kind of rejection that was so much a part of show business. She also wondered what happened when a once much-in-demand youngster woke up to discover that the offers were no longer rolling in. In the two years she had been working in New York, she'd seen several very "hot" kid stars cool off abruptly as they sprouted awkwardly into adolescence. She had actually heard one agent refer to a twelve-year-old as "washed up."

And then there were the parents! Chris had told her frankly when she'd started working for him that stage mothers—and fathers—ranked as one of the major occupational headaches of the industry. Allie had quickly decided that he'd understated the situation.

The three youngsters who would be the principal "spokeschildren" for the new snack products not only had to be telegenic, able to speak lines, and handle direction; they also had to have some genuine athletic ability. For this reason, the last round of auditions— the final callbacks—were conducted in a gymnasium.

Although all the people running the casting call were consummate professionals, it was Allie who kept the session from dissolving into utter pandemonium. Her secret for maintaining control was a slightly dented coach's whistle that was capable of producing a singularly ear-piercing sound.

"Allie, you are a genius," Chris congratulated her after they'd finally finished up with all two dozen of their finalists. "I take back all the nasty things I ever said about your obsessive behavior. The whistle was inspired. If you want, I'll have it bronzed. Better yet, I'll get it gold-plated and engraved at Tiffany's." Before she realized his intention, he was giving her an enthusiastic bear hug, lifting her a few inches off the floor.

"I'll settle for some aspirin and a stiff drink." She laughed, emerging from the embrace a bit unsteadily. The brief but intimate press of body against body had stirred her more than she cared to admit. She made a show of patting her ponytailed hair into order. She'd worn a leotard and tights under her usual working outfit of jeans and a tailored but attractive shirt, and she was very aware of her physical reaction to his nearness.

"How about a throat lozenge?" Elliot Warner inquired in a jocular tone. As the ad agency executive in charge of the snack-food account, he played a key role in the casting for the commercial spots. "You've got to be a little hoarse after all the yelling you've done today, Allie. Tell me, were you a Marine drill instructor or something before you came to Strictly Commercial?" He showed a set of even white teeth.

Allie smiled, her mind replaying the comment Chris had made about Elliot undressing her with his eyes.

As far as she could tell, there was nothing out of the ordinary—certainly nothing salacious—about the way he was looking at her now. Then again, Allie had learned that she wasn't especially good at picking up on male-female undercurrents. Still, the idea of Elliot Warner fantasizing about her, naked, was just too farfetched to consider. Chris had probably been projecting his own highly sexed nature onto the other man.

Had Chris ever fantasized about her . . . naked? Had he ever fantasized about her at all?

"Actually," Allie said, clearing her throat, "my father used to be a high-school athletics director."

"Oh, I see." Elliot nodded. "That helps explain why you were so good at handling all the boys today."

"She's not bad at handling men, either," Chris commented blandly, dropping a companionable arm around her shoulders. The blandness of his tone—to say nothing of his touch—earned him a sharp look from Allie. He simply looked back at her, brows slightly raised. "Are you, Allie?"

Allie shook off his arm, then turned her attention back to Elliot. "I grew up with three older brothers," she explained lightly. "They taught me a lot about handling boys . . . and men. Including"—here she glanced limpidly at Chris—"*including* how to fight dirty."

Elliot chuckled appreciatively, apparently taking the exchange between Allie and Chris as a normal part of their bantering, mettlesome working relationship. "In that case, remind me never to get on your bad side." He became more serious. "Look, I take it we're agreed on the kids we want for the spots? The redhead, Tina—"

"Treena," Allie amended.

"Right, Treena. Also, the black kid from the Bronx. And Henry the Handstander. I just hope those two front teeth of his don't grow in too quickly. The gap is terrific."

"I have the feeling Henry's charming mother would be willing to keep him semi-toothless forever if the price was right," Chris commented sardonically.

Elliot grimaced. "You're probably right."

"Don't worry," Allie said sweetly. "If you think I'm good at handling boys, you should see Chris handle their moms."

"Sure. I'll blow in her ear and murmur the word *residuals* and she'll be eating out of my hand," Chris retorted.

"Is *that* how you do it?" Allie asked innocently, feeling unusually exhilarated by this verbal fencing. She and Chris had always teased each other a great deal, but seldom in such a provocative, double-edged style.

"I'll give you a demonstration sometime," he promised. "When do you think you should have final casting approval from the client on this?" he asked Elliot.

"The end of the week, I hope. We'll screen the videotapes for them tomorrow."

"We're okay on the initial locations?" Chris questioned, running down the checklist of details. While he had been hired as director and chief cameraman for the series of commercials, Strictly Commercial, Inc. was the production company for the enterprise. This meant handling not only casting, but location, props, and wardrobe as well.

"I think we must have Polaroided every playground and school gym on the East Coast," Allie commented wryly, referring to the snapshots taken of potential shooting locations. Strictly Commercial had several file drawers full of photographs—all carefully annotated with light and exposure-angle information—

to help in the selection of shooting sites. Some pictures had been taken for specific commercials. Others were more general, falling into categories like "middle-class suburban kitchen," "upscale urban apartment," or Allie's personal favorite: "all-American house with white picket fence."

"We're fine on the locations," Elliot confirmed. "That playground you picked really reads playground."

Allie fought down a bubble of laughter. Out of the corner of her eye, she saw Chris's lips twitch briefly and knew he shared her instinctive amusement at Elliot's use of ad-industry jargon. Everyone in the business was forever talking about locations or situations or people "reading" a certain way. It was essentially a code word for a subjective judgment, of course. Allie had once heard a story about an agency executive who had jokingly suggested Buckingham Palace as a potential location for a commercial touting a new "regally luxurious" limousine only to be tartly informed that the site simply didn't *read* royalty!

"It's the swings and seesaws that do it," Chris agreed.

"Right." Elliot nodded. "Okay, then, we'll touch base at the end of the week to finalize the casting."

There was a quick round of good-byes and hand-shakes, and then the ad agency people took their leave.

"That whistle really was a brilliant idea," Chris repeated, smiling at Allie.

"I do my best." She was pleased by the compliment.

"Did you just happen to have it lying around your apartment, or am I going to see it under 'Miscellaneous' on your next expense account?"

She resisted the urge to stick her tongue out at him. "As a matter of fact, it was a present from my brother J.J."

"Oh?"

"He gave it to me when I moved to Manhattan. He said I could use it to ward off potential muggers and rapists."

"Do me a favor. Keep it handy if Elliot ever asks you for a date. He reads lecher to me."

Allie rolled her eyes, stuffing a stack of notes, résumés, and photographs into the roomy canvas tote she used instead of a briefcase. "My God, you're not going to start with that nonsense again! And speaking of nonsense, just what was the meaning of your crack about my being able to handle men?"

"I was simply making an observation."

"Oh, right. Honestly, Chris, I don't know where you got the ridiculous idea that Elliot Warner is secretly lusting after me, but you're so far off base it isn't funny. For Pete's sake, he wanted to know if I'd been a *drill instructor!*"

"He was trying to show you he has a sense of humor."

Allie spread her hands helplessly. "You're impossible, do you know that? Look, I grant you I tend to be a little socially dense sometimes—"

"'A *little* socially dense'?" Chris repeated, an unexpected spark of anger flaring in his expressive green eyes. "Allie, you are so oblivious to your effect on men, it's frightening!"

Her mouth dropped open. She shut it after a moment. "What effect on what men?" she demanded, putting her hands on her hips.

Chris looked away for a few seconds, taking a deep breath and visibly shifting emotional gears. "Never mind," he said finally, a curiously frustrated quality edging his words.

"But—" The beginnings of a frown pleated the smooth skin of her high forehead.

"Just forget I said anything." It was a tone that

brooked no further challenge. "It's been a long day. We're both tired, and you're probably hungry. Maybe we can scout up a few of the client's nutritious yet delicious snacks for you."

"No, thanks," she declined politely, still puzzling over his previous statement.

Chris glanced at his watch, his sensually carved lips compressed into a line. "How about getting some dinner, then?" he asked.

Allie blinked. "Don't you have a date or something?" she countered, still off-balance enough to take refuge in uncharacteristic bitchiness. "I thought you were all hot and heavy with Phyllis what's-her-name. The brewery heiress."

"Phyllis is in Paris for the couture collections."

"Ah. She stands you up so she can replenish her wardrobe, and you want me to stand in for her—temporarily, of course."

"All I want, Allie, is to have you answer a simple question." His voice was silken smooth, a potentially dangerous sign. "Do you want to get a bite to eat with me? Yes or no."

"Is this Dutch treat?"

He stared at her. Allie bit her lip. She might be oblivious to the effect she had on most men, but it wasn't hard to see that *this* man wanted to strangle her . . . or worse.

"I'll tell you what," he said slowly, the lean planes of his tanned face setting stubbornly. "Since we've got another, oh, twenty minutes or so on our rental of this damned gym, bring out that basketball you had the kids dribbling around earlier and let's shoot some free throws. Best out of ten wins. The loser springs for dinner."

In her senior year of high school, Allison Anne Douglas had set a state record for free-throw completions in women's varsity basketball that was still unbroken.

On this particular evening, however, she got stuck with the dinner check.

Chapter

3

ANTIGUA DEFINITELY "READ" tropical paradise: it was
a Caribbean dream. Within ten minutes of setting foot
on the beautiful island, Allie was thoroughly en-
chanted. By the time they neared the conclusion of
their two-and-a-half-day shoot, she was contemplating
deserting the fast-paced urban delights of the Big Apple for a career as a beachcomber.

"It's a gorgeous island, isn't it?" Martine Lurie
asked in her distinctive, throaty voice. She was the
star of the perfume commercial they were filming.
Ebony-haired and sloe-eyed, with a faintly exotic cast
to her exquisite features, Martine was one of the love-
liest women Allie had ever seen. She was also one of
the most professional and genuinely nice people she'd
ever worked with.

"Gorgeous," Allie agreed.

"Jon brought me here for an illicit rendezvous one week before we were married," Martine confided with a delicious laugh. "I think I fell in love with Antigua then—or at least with what I could see of it from the window of our hotel suite."

"I take it you didn't get to explore many of the local tourist attractions," Allie surmised.

Martine smiled with a wicked sparkle. "I was too busy exploring Jon's attractions."

Martine was happily married to Jon Norris St. Vincent, an international financier. She'd been a very successful model prior to her marriage four years before. Now, except for a few selective and high-paying assignments, she devoted herself to her husband and her two-year-old daughter, Lucinda.

They were filming the commercial on the east coast of Antigua. The sky overhead was a vivid sapphire dotted with fluffy free-form clouds. It was a perfect complement for the intense, peacock blue of the ocean. Coconut palms lined the glistening white beach where they were shooting. The weather was sunny and dry, the temperature in the balmy 70's.

Except for a few minor problems stemming from the islanders' unshakable conviction that life should be conducted "slowly, slowly," the production had gone without a hitch. They were now taking a brief break before shooting the final close-up they needed. The mood was basically relaxed but ready.

While Allie was talking with Martine, Chris was engaged in a conversation with several members of his crew. The rapport he had with the men—and the respect they had for him—was obvious even at a distance.

Predictably, the shoot had attracted something of a crowd. Martine, who was stunning in a floating

gown of turquiose and white, was the object of much
interest. Chris was coming in for a great deal of attention, too. Considering the way he was dressed—
a pair of brief white swim trunks, another one of his
garish floral-print shirts, and a New York Mets base-
ball cap—Allie wasn't surprised that people, particularly women, were looking at him.

He was magnificently male and arrogantly at ease
as he went about his job, demanding and getting the
best from everyone involved. Allie felt a powerful,
almost painful, surge of emotion as her eyes followed
him.

"Your husband called last night, didn't he?" Allie
asked Martine, trying not to stare. Chris's shirt was
completely unbuttoned. It flapped open in the breeze
to reveal his chest and the flat plane of his stomach.
The white trunks, which rode low on his lean hips
and contrasted vividly with his tanned skin, left very
little to the imagination.

"That's right," Martine said, a shrewd expression
settling over her lovely face as she studied Allie from
beneath her long, slightly lowered lashes.

Allie tore her gaze away from Chris, sighing heavily. "Is everything all right with the international monetary system?" she inquired.

Martine flicked open a compact and checked her
reflection. "The international monetary system is
holding up, but Cinda's got the sniffles and Jon is
positively beside himself. I'm surprised he hasn't called
in a horde of Swiss specialists. He's probably driven
the baby's pediatrician berserk by now. I just hope
he doesn't hound her nanny too much."

Allie had never met Martine's husband, but she
had read about him in the business sections of many
newspapers and magazines. "I can't quite imagine
that," she commented.

Martine shut the compact. "What? You can't imagine Jon Norris St. Vincent as a doting daddy? Believe me, Allie, you're not alone. Even I've been a trifle surprised. Of course, I was surprised when he asked me to marry him, too, given his reputation. But then, isn't there some old saying about reformed rakes making the best husbands?"

"I think it has something to do with them finding the right woman to do the reforming."

"What a nice thing to say!" Martine responded, accepting the sincerely voiced compliment with an appreciative smile. "And speaking of reforming rakes," she said, giving Allie a quizzical glance: "what's with you and Chris?"

"What's with us?" Allie flushed. "Nothing. Why?"

"Well, for one thing, every time you're not looking at him, he's looking at you."

"Martine—"

"Besides which, Parrish Williams told me I should keep an eye on you two."

"Parrish! It's bad enough that *he's* always sticking his nose into everyone else's business. What's he doing now—recruiting for his own intelligence-gathering network? The C.I.A. must be shaking in its shoes." Allie was aware that she was overdoing it just a little. Brittle repartee was not really her style, but Martine's comment had been disconcertingly on target.

"I did a session for *Vogue* last week," Martine explained serenely. "You know, one of those 'It's August so we have to shoot the January fur layout right now' kind of things. In a way, it's better than shivering through a swimsuit shoot in February, which I've done more than once in my career. In any case, Parrish was doing the makeup, and when I mentioned I was coming to Antigua to do this perfume commercial with you and Chris, he said he thought there was something brewing between the two of you."

Allie shook her head. "Chris and I have known each other for two years, Martine. Don't you think if something was 'brewing' between us, it would have come to a boil a long time ago?"

"Sometimes these things take time," the model observed, tilting her head slightly.

"And sometimes these things are all in the mind of a gossip-crazed makeup artist. I think I may send him a poison-pen letter written in eyebrow pencil. Why does Parrish have to pick on me, of all people?" Allie frowned, shifting her weight.

"Parrish wasn't picking on you, Allie. He likes you. A great many people in our business like you, in case you hadn't noticed." Her throaty voice was gently sympathetic, yet sweetly amused.

Allie kicked at the hot white sand with her toe, wondering, horrified, why she suddenly felt like bursting into tears.

"Thanks. Just call me Allison Douglas, everybody's pal," she returned in a small, tight voice.

"Allie!" Chris called from about forty feet away. He was shading his face with one hand as he looked back at her. "Come on, Brown Eyes, let's get this show on the road."

Allie sighed. "Time to sell perfume, Martine," she said.

Several hours later Allie was sitting on the bed in her beachfront hotel room, discontentedly debating her options. Martine was en route back to Manhattan in a plane owned by the cosmetics company. The crew—scheduled for a morning flight the next day—was off somewhere celebrating the successful wrap-up of the shoot. Allie didn't know where Chris was.

It's Friday night in Paradise, she told herself. You

are not going to spend the evening curled up in bed with a book! Consider the possibilities.

She could go down to the hotel's bar and indulge in one of its justifiably famous fruit-and-rum drinks. She could hitch a ride to St. John's, Antigua's colorful capital, and explore the night life. Or, she could order an extravagant meal to eat on her own private patio and then take a leisurely stroll on the beach.

Somehow, none of these ideas seemed terribly appealing.

Sighing, Allie flopped back on the bed like a rag doll, her freshly washed hair spilling over the pillow in a silken wave. She was wearing nothing but a thin, white cotton robe that stopped a few inches short of her knees. Restlessly, she rolled over on her side and propped herself up on one elbow.

"This," she announced, "is ridiculous!"

Someone knocked at the door, and Allie sat up.

There was another knock. "Allie?"

Allie's heart gave a peculiar lurch. "Wait a minute," she called, scrambling off the bed. She crossed to the door and stood, her hand hovering over the knob. "Who is it?" she asked unnecessarily.

"Chris. Who else would it be? Or are you expecting somebody?"

"Of course not!"

"Open up, Allie."

"Why should I?"

"So I can come in," he replied with exaggerated patience. "Unless, of course, I'm interrupting some—"

Allie yanked the door open, her eyes flashing at the drawling emphasis he put on the word *interrupting*.

Chris was standing nonchalantly in the hall, grinning smugly. His outrageously casual attire of earlier in the day had been replaced by impeccable white linen trousers and a custom-tailored navy-blue blazer.

"I figured that would get you to open the door," he told her. His expression changed as he took in her general state of undress. The retort Allie was about to make died in her throat as he reached out and very gently stroked a strand of her loosened hair.

She felt the butterfly-light touch down to the slender soles of her bare feet, and she took a small step backward. "What do you want?" she inquired less than graciously.

"To take you to dinner."

Her eyes widened.

"*If* you don't have any previous plans," he elaborated. "And no, you're not a stand in for anybody else and I don't expect you to pay your own way." His dark brows had come together and there was unmistakable irritation in his voice.

For a moment Allie bristled at his manner. She was tempted to slam the door in his handsome face. Then, without warning, she caught a flash of something— uncertainty? vulnerability?—in Chris's deep-green eyes. Her temper cooled with the realization that, for the first time, she was seeing a Christian Cooper who wasn't totally in control and absolutely sure of himself.

"Well, if you put it that way," she said quietly, "how can I say no?"

Although he relaxed slightly at this, Chris's edginess did not completely disappear. "Are you sure?"

Allie met his eyes steadily, a slow smile curving her lips. "Very," she said, wondering fleetingly why she felt as though she'd just made one of the most important decisions of her life.

She joined him in the hotel bar twenty minutes later. It had only taken her five minutes to slip on a sarong-style dress of coral-and-cream cotton and to thrust her feet into a pair of strappy sandals. The remaining time had been uncharacteristically spent studying her reflection in the bathroom mirror and fussing over her appearance.

The dress—tucked into her suitcase as an afterthought—was a favorite of Allie's. It required a minimum of undergarments and was extremely comfortable to wear. As she put it on, Allie found herself wishing her taste ran to sexier, more stylish outfits. She was virtually oblivious to the way the sarong flattered and subtly underscored the slim curves of her body. She was also unaware of the provocative contrast between the sensuous, undisciplined tumble of her hair and the fine-boned strength of her slightly angular features.

Chris rose lithely as Allie approached him, flashing her a brilliant smile of welcome. There was the faintest hint of relief in the smile. Allie had the astonishing impression that he hadn't been entirely certain she was going to show up.

His eyes slid over her with undisguised interest. Allie's anxieties about the way she looked melted in the warmth of his frank and very masculine appreciation.

"Hello," he said evenly, leaning forward to kiss her on the cheek. A prickle of excitement ran through her like a tiny electric charge as his mouth brushed her smooth, sun-gilded skin.

"Hello," she returned, torn between a strange shyness and a sudden blossoming self-assurance.

Chris had been holding one hand behind his back. Now, with a theatrical flourish, he brought it out, palm up. Allie gave a gasp of pleasure as she saw the lovely crimson-and-gold flower he was offering her.

"Oh, it's beautiful!" she said sincerely, taking it from him and sniffing the blossom's heady perfume.

"I'm glad you like it," he told her quietly.

She made a wry face. "I'm not quite sure what to do with it, though," she confessed, inhaling its scent again.

Chris pretended to consider the matter for a moment. "Well, if you put it behind your left ear, it means you're taken. And if you put it behind your right one, it means you're available and looking." He flicked the lobe of each of her ears as he spoke. "Frankly, though"—he plucked the flower from her fingers—"I think you should wear it here."

"Here" was the top of Allie's wrapped and strapless bodice. Before she realized what he intended to do, Chris had deftly placed the blossom in the faintly shadowed cleft between her small breasts. As he withdrew his hand, she instinctively brought one of her own up, brushing her fingertips over the showy, velvet-soft petals.

Allie had always been conscious of Chris's masculine charm. But never having been on the receiving end of it, she hadn't realized just how potent his appeal could be. She was learning fast.

"A drink before dinner?" he asked smoothly, watching her movements with unnerving intensity. "Something cool and refreshing."

How about a cold shower? she suggested to herself a bit wildly. Calm down, girl!

"A drink sounds . . . wonderful," she declared carefully.

Chris had his customary Scotch. Allie enjoyed something called a Pink Pineapple, which carried quite a rum-based kick despite its deceptively pastel appearance and fruit-salad garnish.

Dinner, served in the hotel's impressively appointed dining room, was delicious. Allie devoured a plate of crab claws and lobster, dipping the delectably fresh seafood morsels in a spicy hot sauce or a cool mayonnaise flavored with lime juice and minced ginger. Chris opted for the baked red snapper, served with a rich and unusual sauce made of egg, olives, and capers.

They talked and laughed and flirted. Their conversation was comfortable and spiced with affectionate friendship. It was also punctuated by brief but electric moments of meaningful silence and high-voltage glances. Allie was trembling with an unfamiliar mixture of anticipation and apprehension by the time Chris guided her outside for a walk on the beach.

"I have to take my shoes off," she told him after the first few steps on the sand. The surf was calm this evening, gently lapping the shore rather than pounding at it. The air was rich with the scent of the sea and the fragrance of countless tropical flowers. "Will you look away for a second, please?"

The moon was out, and Allie could clearly see Chris's mouth twitch. "I've seen women take off their shoes before, Allie," he told her.

"I'm sure you have, but I'm going to slip off my pantyhose, too. I don't want to ruin them in the sand. So just turn the other way or shut your eyes."

Chris obliged, and Allie quickly removed her sandals. She then modestly wriggled out of her pantyhose, balling them up and stuffing them in her purse. "All right," she said, making a small adjustment in her dress.

Chris turned back to her. "Is there anything underneath that dress you're wearing?" he asked after a moment, a definite gleam lighting his eyes.

Allie tilted her chin, her hair rippling with the movement of her head. "Just me," she said, an unconscious hint of challenge in her voice. She was suddenly extremely aware of how soft the fabric of the sarong felt against her naked skin. "That's one of the few advantages of being built like a boy," she added deprecatingly.

Normally, that kind of remark drew a mocking response or a laugh from Chris. This time, however, he made an exasperated sound and said, "I've been around a lot more than you have, Brown Eyes, and I haven't seen many boys who are built like you."

Allie shrugged. "You know what I mean, Chris. I'm not exactly every man's fantasy."

"In other words, you're not a cross between Betty Crocker and a *Playboy* centerfold."

She felt a flash of pain. "Something like that," she agreed, and began walking. The sand was warm against her bare feet.

She got about ten yards down the beach before Chris caught her by the arm and turned her around to face him. "Has it ever occurred to you that you don't know very much about men's fantasies?" he asked, his voice slightly husky. His grip on her flesh became a caress. She caught her breath as his fingers trailed slowly down the length of her arm, finally capturing her hand.

"I never claimed to be an expert on fantasies," she replied, pulling away from him.

"And that's a good thing. Because an expert would have realized that you've been starring in most of mine."

"But you said . . . at your beach house, you said you hadn't—you you didn't think of me—us—that way."

He closed the small distance between them. "I was lying to you," he said quietly. Then he added after a pause, "And to myself."

"Chris . . ."

"I'm tired of fantasies, Allie. And I think you are, too."

Her lips parted in instinctive protest. But before she could utter the words she intended to say, Chris had pulled her to him and covered her mouth with his own.

Chapter

4

IT HAD BEEN a long time since Allie had been kissed by a man, but abstinence alone could not account for the fiery blossom of response that flowered within her when Chris's firm masculine lips claimed and caressed her own softly feminine ones.

Surprise overwhelmed what would have been her automatic resistance in the first moments of the kiss— surprise at Chris's behavior and her own. By the time the surprise dissipated, she was too caught up in the swirling vortex of pleasure he aroused in her to do anything but surrender to it with a small whimper of long-denied hunger.

Chris's mouth was gentle at first, teasing and tempting, making sensual promises with seductive expertise. The slow stroke of his hands over her slender body was exploratory yet infinitely knowing. Allie shuddered sweetly as he pulled her more firmly against him and deepened the kiss.

Her lips parted under the coaxing pressure of his and she first accepted, then eagerly sought, the slick thrust of his tongue. The taste of him filled her mouth even as the musk-and-spice scent of his warm skin assailed her nostrils. She arched slightly, dizzily conscious of the softly erotic friction of the wrapped cotton dress against her body.

Chris had no need to take from her; she was more than willing to give. And he clearly wanted more than her passive acceptance of his attentions. When, at some unknowable point in the kiss, she suddenly began making her own demands, he gave a low growl of satisfaction deep in his throat.

Allie's slim, bare arms came up, circling his neck, her fingers threading possessively through the dark tangle of curls at the back of his head. His hair was thick and springy, so very vital in its texture. She went up on tiptoe in the sand, tilting her head back a little, her long, loosened tresses swaying over her shoulders in a curtain of silk.

She wanted this . . . him. It was something she had known for days, weeks, *months*, without ever quite admitting it to herself. She trembled, poised between a delicious sense of the unknown and a heady feeling of déjà vu, as Chris kissed a burning path down the tender line of her throat.

He was the lover she had never had, and yet she felt she knew him as though they'd possessed each other from the beginning of time.

Finally, he lifted his head but did not release her. She trembled a little as his heated gaze moved over her, absorbing the visual essence of her response.

"I feel like I'm drunk on you," he told her huskily.

"The touch of you . . . the scent . . . the taste of your mouth."

Allie gave a soft laugh, a tantalizing mixture of shyness and provocation. "I probably taste like rum and pineapple," she said. "The drink—"

He hushed her with a firm but gentle finger. "No, Allie, don't make a joke out of it. You don't taste of anything but sweet heat and hunger. The same hunger I've got."

He kissed her again, a little harder this time, a little less controlled. Allie responded, her eyes closing as her lips opened to the search of his tongue.

"I want you, Allie," he murmured. "I want to make love with you. Tonight. *Now*. And I can feel the want in you, too, Brown Eyes. Don't deny it."

Her eyelids fluttered open. "I'm not denying it," she returned with unashamed simplicity. How could she deny it when every fiber of her body was yearning to belong to him? Tonight. Now. "I want you, too, Chris."

You always have, a tiny voice said. And she knew it must be true.

Hand-in-hand, they walked back across the warm sand, stopping to kiss, to touch, to affirm what was building between them. There was no need to hurry. It was as though both of them knew that what they were about to do together had been destined and decided a long time before.

They went to Chris's room—his bungalow, really. While the rest of the crew had been given accommodations in the hotel itself, he'd been housed in one of several Haitian-style huts placed a discreet distance from the main building. At this moment, the luxurious privacy that arrangement afforded seemed beautifully, utterly right.

His bedroom was airy, simply furnished, and scrupulously neat. It was bathed in the soft silvery glow of the moon, and Chris made no effort to turn on any artificial lights when they entered.

Allie's heart was pounding with a wild life of its own as they faced each other for a moment, not speaking and not touching. It was a moment, the last of its kind, for pulling back. It was also a moment, the first of its kind, for recognizing that neither of them could pull back—even if he or she had wanted to.

"I think we've been waiting for this for a long time," Chris said, his voice full of rueful wonder.

"I feel like I'm dreaming." That was completely true as far as it went. She also knew that no dream could have the crystalline clarity of this encounter.

One corner of his mouth quirked, and Allie sensed their thoughts intertwined.

"This is no dream," he told her. There was a glinting promise of proofs to come in his compellingly green eyes. He shucked off his blazer and carelessly tossed it aside, then slowly began unbuttoning his shirt.

With excitement fizzing through her veins like electrified champagne, Allie turned away and carefully undid the knot that held her dress in place. The sarong slithered to the floor, puddling around her bare feet in a swirling pool of coral and cream. With her head bowed slightly and her tawny tumble of hair spilling forward to veil her delicate breasts, she turned back.

Her breath caught at the top of her throat as she took in his masculine nudity. The silvered glow of moonlight flooding into the room underscored the classic, somehow pagan quality of his lean yet unmistakably powerful body. She drank him in with her eyes, celebrating, in trembling anticipation, the strength of the desire she saw in him.

She experienced a moment of hesitation, a flash of an all too familiar sense of insecurity as he closed the small distance between them and gently, tenderly, brushed her hair back over her shoulders so he could fondle the soft swell of her small breasts. A shaft of pleasure lanced through her as he teased one rosy peak with his thumb, his lips curving as the sensitive bit of flesh sprang erect.

"You see what I meant about my being built like a boy," she said, trying for a casual, flippant tone and missing. Anxiety and an odd sort of apology were clear in her words and her voice.

Chris muttered something under his breath that sounded like a curse, his brows drawing together for a split second. Then his expression cleared and he transferred his tactile ministrations to her other breast.

"Haven't you ever heard the phrase 'More than a handful is wasted'?" he queried in a deep, velvety voice, his fingers working their blood-heating magic on her body. Allie flushed suddenly and made a small sound as he cupped both of her breasts in his hands, treasuring their delicate, firm-skinned roundness. "See how well you fit in my palms?" He moved closer to her. "And you can feel how well we'll fit together, can't you, Allie?"

"Y-yes!" she gasped.

Bending his head, he kissed her again. They savored each other's mouths hungrily. She parted her lips to the coaxing probe of his tongue and felt him trace the rim of her teeth before he plunged inward, taking possession of the sweetly moist hollow of her mouth.

His hands stroked her torso, the faintly roughened tips of his fingers sending delicious tingles of pleasure darting through her. His palms molded the slim curves of her hips, before slipping around to languidly massage her buttocks for a moment. Then, with a throaty groan, he swept her up into his arms like a whirlwind and set her down on the bed with infinite, cherishing, care.

He didn't tell her that her features were beautiful or that her body was voluptuous, but his expressive eyes clearly revealed how very, very desirable he found her.

He stretched out beside her, his lean-molded face set and his breathing carefully controlled as though he was holding himself in check. Allie reached for him, touching with an intuitive boldness that made him shudder and exhale with a sudden groan.

"Allie..." he caught her wandering hand, stilling it against the throbbing evidence of his arousal. The heat and power of him, of his response to her, affected Allie like the most potent of aphrodisiacs.

He wooed her with increasing urgency, feasting on the yielding sweetness of her mouth and searching out the secrets of her passion with unerring skill. Allie trembled, moving against him as he explored her body with his lips and hands, teaching her what she was and could be in the same soaring moments he discovered for himself.

He gave her far more than pleasure, and she answered him with an ardor that went way beyond sexual willingness.

He kissed a searing trail down her throat, then sought the nipple of her right breast with his mouth. He sucked the taut coral tip with erotic appetite, his tongue teasing and tormenting. He paid the same tantalizing homage to her other breast, nibbling gently at her quivering flesh.

Allie felt herself blossoming under his attentions, her body growing moist and pliant. She scored a wanton path down his spine with her nails, listening to his throaty exclamation of response with greedy relish. She moaned in turn as his deft fingers stroked between her thighs, pleasuring and preparing her with tender expertise.

Half of her wanted to indulge herself and prolong these preliminary delights as long as possible, to sate her body in this very passionate mating game. The other half wanted to hurtle forward toward the moment of ultimate, explosive union.

She rocked her hips in languid but unmistakable invitation. Chris shifted, the press of his maleness throbbing against her. Their individual rhythms met, matched, then effortlessly merged.

It was only at the last second, when Chris knelt between her thighs, that Allie experienced a hint of fear. It was only a flash, a niggling doubt...

But Chris sensed it in the sudden, subtle ripple of tension that ran through her. He felt the apprehension as well as the anticipation in her straining body.

"Don't be afraid," he whispered hoarsely, stroking her hair and raining quick, urgent kisses on her up-turned face. "It will be good for you, Allie, I promise."

And then they came together; the raging torrent of their mutual desire drowning all doubts and uncertainties. He possessed her utterly, undeniably—like a force of nature. She clung to him, locked heart to heart, surrendering herself with rapturous abandon, to wave after wave of ecstatic sensation. Then the rushing tide of their passion finally crested, and Allie knew completion.

Adam had never liked to talk after they made love. Chris, she discovered, apparently felt the same way. She'd started to speak as they lay together, their yielding, perspiration-slick bodies still intertwined, but he'd hushed her with a long, lingering kiss. He'd then shifted her gently against him, settling her possessively in the cradle of his arms, and told her to sleep.

The words Chris had stopped her from saying hadn't been particularly profound, Allie thought, a little defensively. She hadn't been on the verge of any great emotional declaration or demand for commitment. All she'd wanted to do, she told herself, was to prolong the mood of intimacy, to get some assurance that what had just happened between them was as important to him as it was to her.

Chris woke her twice during the night. The first time he took her with almost primitive simplicity, rousing her from sleep to basic, aching need in a matter of minutes, then fulfilling her in a fashion that was as dominating as it was devastatingly satisfying. The second time, his kisses and caresses took on a dreamy, drugging quality, and Allie felt herself floating somewhere between fantasy and reality as they merged with languid, lingering deliberation.

It was the dawning realization that she was alone in bed that woke her the third time. She sat up slowly, her honeyed hair tumbling in disorderd waves over her back and shoulders. In an unthinking movement, she drew the rumpled bed linen up to cover her nakedness. The sheets were warm and still carried Chris's scent.

She wasn't simply alone in Chris's bed; she was alone in his *room*. The bungalow was quiet. Empty. Her eyes wide with bewilderment and more than a trace of apprehension, Allie looked around.

She stiffened as she heard the click of a key turning in the door. Clutching the sheets tightly around her, she sat up as straight as she could. "Chris?" she asked.

The door swung open. "You'd better not be expecting anybody else at this time of the morning," Chris's smooth voice informed her.

He came in wearing jeans and a white knit shirt that fit like a second skin. He was carrying her garment bag and overnight tote. Draping the bag over a chair and dumping the tote down beside it, he surveyed her with interest.

Allie blinked, smothering a yawn with the back of her hand. What on earth was he doing with her luggage?

"What time is it?" she asked, still clinging to the sheets. You're not hiding anything he hasn't already seen, a little voice piped up mockingly.

He glanced at his watch and told her. Allie gasped.

"But it can't be! The plane—"

"—left about twenty minutes ago. With everyone and everything safely on board."

"Except us."

He walked toward her. "I canceled our reservations. We're going back on Tuesday."

Allie swallowed hard, staring at him in disbelief as he sat down on the edge of the bed. He was so *casual,* acting as if he did this sort of thing all the time.

Maybe, she thought with a pang, he does.

Well, Allison Anne Douglas didn't. She bent her head slightly. It seemed the morning after the night before had arrived with a vengeance.

"Allie?" Chris questioned, hooking two fingers under her chin and tilting her face up.

She swallowed. "When did you make up your mind about our not going back until Tuesday?" she asked. A horrible thought occurred to her. Could all of this have been planned? She knew that Chris had specifically requested the bungalow. Had he been intending this all along?

"Early this morning," he replied, studying her through slightly narrowed eyes. "I know I should have woken you up and asked you, but you looked so peaceful sleeping there." He shrugged in rueful and apparently genuine apology.

Allie relaxed a little, the knot of doubt that had formed around her heart loosening. She nibbled her lower lip, trying to sort out her feelings. On the one hand, she was deeply relieved that Chris wasn't treating this like a one-night stand; but, on the other, she wasn't at all certain of what she was getting herself into. What had happened the night before had shaken her perspective about a lot of things.

"I suppose you know what everybody's going to think now, don't you?"

Chris's well-shaped mouth twisted wryly. "I've got news for you, Brown Eyes. It's not a matter of what they're *going* to think. They've been thinking it for some time."

"What?" The word came out an octave above her normal tone of voice.

"It seems there's been more than the usual speculation about the two of us in recent weeks."

"Where did you hear that?"

"Parrish."

"Parrish!"

"Hey, take it easy." He stroked one palm down the side of her neck, soothing her agitation. His hand moved to her bare shoulder, massaging lightly, comfortingly. "As unlikely as it may sound, our big-mouthed makeup artist has not been gossiping. But he told me that other people have been."

"Why in heaven's name?" Allie demanded.

"For one thing, we haven't exactly been acting normally around each other lately," he said flatly, then raised his brows significantly as though inviting her to remember a number of their recent exchanges.

"But—"

"Actually," he went on dryly, "the last time I saw

Parrish, he wanted to know what my intentions toward you were."

Allie groaned. Drawing her legs up underneath the sheet, she buried her hot face against her knees. "I'm not even going to ask what you told him," she responded. Her voice was muffled enough so the unsteadiness in it was not too noticeable.

There was a pause.

"Allie," Chris said finally. "Allie, look at me."

After a moment, she obeyed. Her face was slightly flushed, and there was a mixture of mutiny and vulnerability in the set of her mouth and chin.

"Do you really care what people are going to think?" he asked quietly. "Or is it the fact that we've become lovers you're having trouble coping with?"

Allie tensed visibly, feeling herself put on the spot.

"It's not that . . ." She hesitated, her eyes darting away from his. She'd been honest with Chris about so many things in the past. Why was it suddenly so hard to tell him the truth about what she was feeling now? She took a deep breath and let it out. "It's just that after two years of being one of the few women you *hadn't* slept with, it takes a little adjustment to get used to the idea of being . . . you know—one of the crowd."

She regretted the last four words even as they were leaving her mouth. The whole thing sounded a lot more insulting—to both of them—than she had intended. She winced inwardly, still not daring to look at him.

Chris remained silent for what seemed like a very, very long time. As the silence lengthened, Allie felt something inside her dying off by inches. She realized, with a painful flash of insight, that she desperately wanted him to tell her that she wasn't just one of the crowd. She needed him to reassure her that even though she had gone to bed with him, the relationship they'd built up over the past two years wasn't going to change.

He sighed. It was a long, weary-sounding exhalation. Oh Lord, Allie thought, feeling a little sick. He must think I'm trying to trap him into some kind of commitment.

"Allie," he began slowly. "Look—"

"No, Chris, it's okay," she cut in hastily. "I was only joking. I didn't mean that the way it came out. It's just that I haven't had a lot of experience with this sort of thing."

Oh, now that was a really bright thing to say, she chided herself angrily. Steeling herself, she met his gaze. It was impossible to tell what he was thinking, and Allie wasn't sure she wanted to know.

He traced the line of her cheek carefully with one finger, his touch light and gentle. "I'm the first man you've been with since your divorce, aren't I." It was a statement, not a question.

Is it that obvious? Allie asked herself derisively. Had she been too eager, too much the desperate divorcée? Or had she been too inexperienced? She nodded her head once.

"You think last night was a mistake, don't you?" she said, fighting to keep the plaintiveness out of her voice.

While his mouth curved into a smile, the expression did not touch his eyes. "How could anything that felt so good be a mistake?" he asked.

It was an indication of how unsettled Allie was that she did not immediately realize he'd evaded her question. By the time his remark registered and she'd opened her mouth to protest, Chris was speaking again.

"Allie, I understand that this is a little strange for you, really, I do. It's not exactly easy for me, either."

"But I—"

"But we both know that something's been going on between us lately. It's not the same. Working together, hanging around together"—he gestured a little helplessly—"it's been different, Allie. Not necessarily better or worse, but different."

"So?" she asked in a small voice.

"So, I'm hoping that if we can spend a few days with each other, alone, away from all the usual madness, we can work this through. Get things straightened out."

Allie stared at him for several seconds. He sounded so reasonable, so damned offhand about the whole situation! He'd turned her world upside down the night before, and now he was calmly talking about "working this through"!

And yet . . . was what he seemed to be driving at so terrible? All right, after two years of a wonderful, platonic friendship, she and Chris had suddenly developed an unexpected sexual attraction and, being consenting adults, they'd given in to it. But that didn't mean the fabric of their two-year relationship had to change, did it? Wasn't she being a little melodramatic? They'd both caught a . . . fever, and here she was acting as though they'd developed a terminal condition!

Wasn't she opening herself up to inevitable hurt and rejection by trying to turn one night of lovemaking into something more than one night of lovemaking? Wasn't she trying to turn *herself* into something she wasn't? Hadn't that very thing been at the root of so many of her problems with Adam?

It's an infatuation, that's all, Allie told herself firmly. This is an interlude, nothing more. Even if Chris were looking for a long-term involvement—and he's not—you'd hardly fit the bill. You're going to wind up being his ex-lover, no matter what else happens. If you mishandle this, you'll end up being his ex-friend as well.

When Allie spoke again, she chose her words with care. "What you're saying is that you think we should let nature take its course. You think that whatever it is that's going on between us will wear itself—burn itself—out. And when it does, we can go back to the way things used to be."

Chris nodded. Allie could have sworn he looked relieved.

"And, in the meantime . . ." she began tentatively.

"In the meantime, we've got the sun, the sand, and four days all to ourselves. Let's enjoy them together, Brown Eyes."

Four days, Allie repeated silently, tingling with an odd combination of pleasurable expectation and anxious dread. Four days all to ourselves.

Yes, she'd enjoy them with him. And when they were over, she and Chris would go back to the way things had always been.

At least Chris would go back. Allie had the sudden suspicion that it wouldn't be so easy for her. "The way things used to be" hadn't included the realization that she was in love with Christian Cooper.

"So, what do you say we just forget about the Big Apple rat race and stay here for the rest of our lives?" Chris asked with a lazy grin as they lingered over dessert at a late lunch Monday afternoon. Antigua offered an enchanting variety of restaurants, and they had yet to eat at the same place twice.

They'd been drawn to this particular dining room at a small hotel on Callaloo Beach after a long, ambling morning of shell collecting and sunbathing. They'd feasted on homemade soups—garden-fresh gazpacho for Allie, a creamy chilled pumpkin bisque for Chris—and oven-warm bread, then allowed themselves to be tempted by the pastry cart.

Allie nearly choked on a mouthful of the refreshingly tart lime pie she was swallowing. Although she knew perfectly well that Chris was teasing, she could not prevent her heart from turning over in response to his casual, joking suggestion.

Chris pushed his untouched glass of ice water across the table to her. "Drink some," he counseled. "It'll clear your throat. Or do you want me to perform the Heimlich maneuver on you?"

Allie did as he instructed. The danger of her choking on the rich yet airy pie had passed, but she was grateful for the chance to collect herself.

"Thank you," she said finally, her voice a trifle huskier than usual.

He leaned back in his seat, surveying her from beneath partially lowered lids. "You don't see me as a full-time beach bum, hmm?" he questioned lightly, running his fingers back through his hair.

Allie smiled at him. "Well, you do look the part," she conceded. Like most of the other patrons in the dining room, they were very casually dressed. Both of them were wearing shorts and Sea Island cotton shirts they had purchased on impulse in a shop they'd wandered into while exploring St. John's. Chris's tan had deepened during the past few days, and his dark hair had picked up a few reddish-gold glints from the sun. His lean features were relaxed, and there was a gleam of mischief in his mesmerizing green eyes as he looked at her.

"But?" he prompted, one brow going up. His gaze moved slowly, deliberately, to her slightly parted lips, then back to her eyes.

"But—" Allie took another sip of water, feeling her bones turn to jelly; Chris had to know what he was doing to her!—"I can't quite see you going from being the King of Commercials to collecting coral for a living."

"Ah."

"You might be all right for—oh, maybe a month or so, but then you'd get the itch again."

"And what itch might that be, Brown Eyes?" he inquired politely. His eyes wandered downward again, this time including her breasts in his provocative inspection.

Allie fiddled with her rather untidily ponytailed hair, twisting a tawny strand around several fingers. The unmistakably sexual undercurrents in this conversation made her both excited and uneasy. This type of verbal fencing was exhilarating and arousing here and now, but what was going to happen when they returned to New York and went back to the way things "used to be"? Were words suddenly going to stop having the kind of erotic double meanings they'd been discovering over the last three days? Was the electricity of Chris's voice . . . his look . . . his touch . . . going to lose its power over her?

"I suppose you're going to try to tell me you weren't thinking about work last night when we were walking along the beach at sunset?" she jibed, flipping her hair back over her shoulder. "I know that intense expression of yours, Christian Cooper. I was half expecting you to whip out a light meter and call for a camera setup. You were thinking about making a commercial, weren't you?"

Chris's obvious preoccupation the evening before had shaken Allie more than she wanted to admit. While, in her insecurity, she had forced herself to accept the reality that there was no way she was going to hold Chris's sexual interest for long, she'd been hurt to find his attention wandering from her after only seventy-two hours. Preparing herself to deal with the inevitable had done absolutely nothing to reduce the pain of it.

"If you'll forgive my bluntness, Allie," Chris said flatly, "the only thing I was thinking about *making* last night was love to you."

Allie's breath caught at the top of her throat and she dropped her eyes, afraid of how revealing her reaction to his words might be. Yes, she could forgive his bluntness. In fact, a part of her thrilled to his frank admission of desire. And yet...

And yet, he'd made the admission so smoothly— *too* smoothly. The veteran of scores of affairs, Chris knew exactly what needed to be said and how to say it. He was a master of the art of flirtation; a man who could soothe or seduce with a few well-chosen words.

Chris had no need to choose his words with Allie before coming to Antigua. She took no pleasure in the realization that he apparently thought he had to begin doing so now.

Allie knew, no matter what he'd just told her, that he'd had something far more consuming than love-making on his mind the night before: something he wouldn't—or couldn't—share with her. The knowledge pierced her like a stake.

"Allie?"

She looked up slowly, praying her expression wouldn't betray what was going on in her heart.

"Are you all right?" he questioned softly, the velvet caress of his concern sending a little quiver running through her.

No, I'm not all right, she thought. I'm in love with you! But you're not in love with me, are you?

"I'm fine, Chris," she lied, not knowing what she would do if he pressed her on the issue.

He hesitated, his eyes narrowing slightly. "Okay,"

he responded after a long moment. Allie wasn't certain whether he meant it was okay that she was fine or that it was okay she'd lied and he was willing to accept her lame falsehood.

She felt a queer, contradictory surge of relief and resentment. On the one hand, she was glad that Chris was letting the subject drop; on the other, she was perversely angry that he hadn't made more of an effort to discover what was so obviously bothering her.

Before Antigua, she told herself unhappily, he would have kept after you until he found out what was wrong. But now...

Chris got up, dropping a crumpled handful of bills on the table to pay for their meal. Allie rose, too.

"You're probably right about me not being the beach-bum type," he observed.

She nodded, summoning up what she hoped was a casual smile. "Well, take heart. In just a little over twenty-four hours we'll be in the Big Apple rat race again, and everything will be back to normal."

"Normal," he repeated with an odd edge of determination.

They spent the remainder of the day exploring Antigua's pride and joy, English Harbour. Once Britain's key naval base in the Caribbean, it had been commanded at one time by the great Horatio Nelson and later by the Duke of Clarence, who was to become William the Fourth of England. Although allowed to fall into shameful disrepair at the turn of the century, it had been restored following World War II. The Harbour and its beautifully rebuilt Dockyard were now justly celebrated within the international yachting fraternity.

Although the historic flavor of the area had been skillfully preserved and enhanced, the Harbour was

first and foremost devoted to modern-day maritime
and commercial activities. The gleaming white boats
that bobbed in the blue-green waters off the docks
proudly bore the markings of at least a dozen different
countries, and the marvelously restored buildings
teemed with a variety of businesses.

Allie enjoyed it all—to a point. There were long
stretches of minutes when she and Chris seemed to
fall back into their easy, blissfully uncomplicated pat-
tern of camaraderie: secure in the unspoken notion
that they were a couple of friends—not simply a couple. But then, without warning, their eyes would meet
or their bodies brush . . .

It's this place, she told herself desperately. The
sun, the sand, the sea. Once we're back in New York,
back at Strictly Commercial, I'll stop reacting this
way.

She'd have to. Chris had made it very clear that
the purpose of these four days together was to work
things through, to get them straightened out. To have
her return to Manhattan behaving like some infatuated
fool wasn't on his agenda. Chris didn't want her—
or any other woman—as a long-term lover.

What he did want was Allison Anne Douglas as
his friend. That Sunday afternoon out on the Hamptons when he'd told her he hadn't thought about having an affair with her, he'd called her his friend as
though the word had a very special meaning for him.
Given all the women in his life, perhaps it did.

I'm a buddy, not a bedmate, Allie thought with a
pang. I should stick to what I'm good at.

That thought lingered, achingly, through a romantic dinner served by candlelight in his—their—bungalow and into the small, dark hours just before dawn.
Chris had been the most attentive, inventive of lovers
during their last night, binding her to him with a

seductive web of sensuality, weaving a hot, hungry spell over body.

Allie's response to him was bold and uninhibited. Guided by the most primitive of instincts, she matched him in demand and generosity. She was greedy and giving in turn, arousing herself and him with an urgency she had never known before. When he finally brought her to release, her pleasure was heightened to a shattering level by the sound of his own hoarse cries of satisfaction and the feel of his proud male body shuddering in climax above hers.

She woke shortly after sunrise to the sound of Chris's deep, measured breathing beside her. His body was curved to shelter hers, and his right arm held her against him. His warm palm cupped one of her breasts, lending the delicate, pink-tipped mound a voluptuousness that Allie had never before appreciated. A tingle of excitement skittered through her, and her nipple stiffened. Chris's arm tightened and he murmured something into her hair.

Allie forced herself to remain very still for several minutes, ignoring the sudden pounding of her pulse and disciplining her breathing. With a tearing sense of regret, she disengaged herself and got out of bed. Slipping into her robe, she tiptoed to the bathroom and shut the door.

There was a large mirror hanging over the sink, and she stared into it silently for a long time. She catalogued the sun-gilded, angular features and the sleep-tumbled honey-colored hair with care, not quite sure what she was searching for. Same old face, she told herself. Same old me.

And yet there was an unfamiliar softness, a new ripeness to her mouth. And the look in her eyes . . .

With a small distressed sound, Allie looked away from the mirror and stripped off her robe. Dropping it carelessly on the cool tile floor, she stepped into the glass-enclosed shower and pulled the door shut behind her. She turned the water on full force. Closing her eyes and trying to will her mind into a merciful blankness, she gave herself up to the pulsing massage of the shower. She tilted her head into the spray, letting the water gush over her face, then down the length of her body.

Allie didn't need to see or hear to know when Chris joined her. Even before his hands slipped around her waist, sliding over her shower-slick skin in an intimate caress and then turning her to face him, she was acutely aware of him. His male presence filled the small glassed-in stall completely.

She opened her eyes, staring up into his face. She trembled a little as he brushed several sodden strands of hair off her cheeks, his fingers teasing the rim of her ear.

"I know I said we had to get going early to catch the plane," he told her with a lazy, blood-heating smile. "But I didn't mean you had to crawl out of bed at the crack of dawn."

She brought her palms up, pressing them flat against his hair-matted chest. She felt, rather than heard, him catch his breath when her fingertips grazed the tight circles of his nipples.

"I couldn't sleep," she told him. The statement was part truth, part invitation.

He took the invitation, his mouth swooping down to cover hers. "Well," he murmured against her lips, "since we're both up . . ."

Allie parted her lips, her tongue darting forward to begin a tantalizing courtship with his. Chris laughed deep in his throat, accepting the sweet advantage she offered with a deliberate, devouring hunger.

His mouth trailed a heated path down her neck,

branding her with kisses and teasing nips. Allie tilted her head back, her fingers gripping his shower-slick shoulders as she felt the warm sweep of his tongue in the delicate cleft between her breasts.

"Chris!" She gasped out his name as his mouth settled on one straining rosebud nipple, suckling briefly, then favored its twin with the same erotic expertise.

"Chris..." Comprehension of what he intended to do washed over her like a cresting wave even before she consciously realized that he had maneuvered her carefully against the wall of the stall and was kneeling before her. The first touch of his mouth was like a torch to tinder, evoking a yearning, fiery response. The second and third nearly caused her knees to buckle. Allie whimpered, shuddering at his intimate invasion.

He held her captive with relentless gentleness, urging her toward total abandonment. Crying out, Allie caught her fingers in his thick, dark hair and tugged. His head lifted slightly.

"Did Adam ever do this to you, Allie?" he asked. The question, spoken unsteadily in a thickened voice, was pitched to cut through the whoosh of the shower and the pounding of her pulse. "Did he?"

Allie's eyes were clenched shut. She was beyond making a coherent reply. She shook her head once.

Chris said something—a single, savage word—against the tender, sensitized skin of her inner thigh. A few moments later, he had the moaning, unbridled surrender he wanted, one that she was only too glad to give.

Chapter

5

THE FLIGHT HOME to New York was uneventful. Allie napped a little, leafed through three magazines she had already read, and chatted with Chris in what she told herself was a perfectly normal manner.

She also accepted—three times—the smiling stewardess's gracious offer of complimentary champagne. Allie sensed that her uncharacteristic imbibing surprised Chris, but since he downed an equal amount of the sparkling wine, plus two Scotches, he was in no position to criticize.

They shared a taxi into the city, just the way they always did when returning from an out-of-town shoot. Chris instructed the driver to go to Allie's address first. The cabbie turned out to be a compulsive talker and, in addition to cursing the near-gridlocked traffic conditions, he kept up a stream of opinionated but amusing dialogue. Allie was grateful to be spared the necessity of making conversation.

"Allie," Chris said with an odd urgency, catching her hand as she reached for the door handle after the cab pulled up in front of her building. The driver had gotten out and was opening the trunk to retrieve her luggage. "Are you all right?"

She pulled her fingers free of his. "Of course I am," she replied. "Why shouldn't I be?"

"I—"

"Are *you* all right?" There's no defense like a good offense, she told herself, recalling one of her father's many athletic-field adages. She didn't want to think about the fact that she suddenly felt the need to defend herself against Chris's questions.

His jaw tightened and his dark brows drew together. "I'm fine."

"Good." She reached for the door handle again. It wouldn't give. She made another effort, meeting with the same lack of success.

Oh, terrific! she thought sardonically. This is all I need!

"It's locked," Chris said quietly, leaning across her to undo the latch. His arm brushed her breasts as he did so. Allie sucked in her breath, biting her lower lip.

"Thank you," she said after a moment, wondering if he had any idea of how his closeness was unnerving her.

"You're welcome," he replied. "Look, uh, do you want me to come up?"

"No!" she blurted out and then flushed, humiliated by her lack of control. She swallowed hard. "I mean . . . do *you* want to come up?"

There was a short silence. Finally, Chris shook his

head with a barely perceptible movement. "No, that's okay. Thanks. I just thought . . . ah, how about a rain-check?"

"Oh, sure, fine," Allie responded with Emily Post-ish propriety. *What* had he just thought?!

"Great." He paused, obviously at a loss for words.

Lord, he's acting like we're a pair of high-school kids just coming home from our first date. Allie re-alized with a kind of dismal humor as her well-developed sense of the absurd reasserted itself with unpredictable and unexpected force. He doesn't know whether to kiss me, shake my hand, or run for his life!

The cabbie opened the door. "Havin' trouble with this?" he asked. "Damn thing's been stickin' on me ever since some jerk from Jersey sideswiped me."

"Thank you," Allie said, fighting down a semi-hysterical desire to start laughing. She glanced at Chris. His expression was on the grim side of unreadable. "I'll see you tomorrow, Chris," she said.

"Tomorrow," he nodded, barely moving his lips as he spoke.

The way he pronounced the word, Allie wasn't certain whether he meant it as a threat or a promise.

She was still uncertain an hour later when, having watered her plants, sorted through her mail, and lis-tened to the calls on her answering machine, she turned to the task of unpacking. It was not a job she normally looked forward to, but now she welcomed anything that would keep her busy, anything that would keep her from thinking and feeling.

Operating on a sort of automatic pilot, Allie un-zipped her overnight tote and opened it up. She gri-maced as she saw the contents.

Usually, Allie was a very neat and organized packer.

After her session in the shower with Chris, however, she hadn't had time to do anything more than stuff her belongings into her luggage and hope she didn't forget anything too important. Staring at the jumble of wrinkled clothes, toiletries, and miscellaneous articles that confronted her now, Allie wondered ruefully if there'd ever been a psychological study correlating a person's state of mind with his or her style of packing.

"What a mess," she muttered, upending the bag with a disgusted grunt. "What—a—*mess!*"

She wasn't just describing the contents of her suitcase.

Allie took several deep breaths, clamping down on the unruly emotions surging up within her. Setting her jaw, she went down on her knees and began picking through the things she had so unceremoniously dumped onto the floor.

"What the—?" she exclaimed suddenly as she fished a small, tissue-wrapped box out of a tangle of underwear. Her name was written on the wrapping in a boldly familiar scrawl.

The box was heavy for its size and rattled a little when she shook it. Frowning, Allie undid the tissue paper. After a moment of hesitation, she lifted the lid—and gasped.

The box contained an utterly exquisite gold bracelet set with white opals and black twig coral. Allie recognized it with a burst of numbed shock. She'd spotted it at a jeweler's atelier while she and Chris were wandering through the shops at English Harbour back on Antigua. Although she was not normally attracted by the gleam of precious metals and the sparkle of gemstones, she'd been genuinely tempted by this one-of-a-kind bangle. The bracelet's hefty price tag—and Chris's sudden and somewhat impatient reminder that they had a dinner reservation to get ready for—had finally weaned her away from what would have been a very uncharacteristic impulse buy.

Her fingers trembling, Allie lifted the beautiful circlet out of its box. The gold had a satiny sheen to it and the opals winked and glowed with a hypnotic inner fire.

" *'The way things used to be...'* " she quoted in a whisper-soft voice.

Whether she meant it as a threat or a promise, Allie didn't know. The only thing she knew was that her automatic pilot had broken down, and she was starting to cry.

Although she never would have admitted it, Allie took extra pains with the way she looked the following day. And it was not just a matter of applying more makeup than usual to mask the signs of a strained and restless night, either. Her normal jeans and tailored top were replaced by a sleek pair of linen slacks, a striped silk shirt in tones of brown and rust, and a sleeveless crocheted vest of cream cotton. Her hair was brushed to a silken gloss and flatteringly pulled back in French plaits.

Donna, Strictly Commercial's stringbean-skinny receptionist, greeted her with a cheery grin. "Welcome back," she said, extending a stack of mail and a sheaf of pink message slips as Allie came through the door. "You look terrific, Allie."

Allie took the proffered material. "Thank you. It's nice to be back."

"I'll bet," Donna returned with a laugh. "No kidding, Allie, you look wonderful. Antigua must have agreed with you."

Allie wondered fleetingly if there was a double meaning in Donna's comment and then decided she was being paranoid. The receptionist wasn't given to sly insinuations. If she had something to say, she came out and said it—no "nudge-nudge, wink-wink" for her.

"It was . . . fun," Allie said after a moment, starting to shuffle through her messages with practiced efficiency.

"You got some sun, I see," Donna observed chattily.

"Uh, yes."

"Chris looks gorgeous, too," the receptionist continued blithely. "Of course, he's got the kind of skin that tans real easily."

Why the big fuss about our color? Allie asked herself. What did she expect? That Chris and I were going to come back from the Caribbean looking as though we'd never seen the light of day?

Allie's stomach knotted. That was probably *just* what Donna had been expecting!

"Allie?" the receptionist asked in a concerned voice.

"What?" Allie countered abruptly, feeling both ashamed and angry.

Donna blinked, visibly surprised. "Hey, are you okay?"

Allie took a deep breath, giving herself a mental shake. She'd known there was bound to be some office reaction to her spending the extended weekend with Chris in Antigua, and she'd thought she was ready to cope with it. Obviously, she'd been wrong. Well, she was going to have to do some quick learning. If she couldn't handle a few friendly questions from Donna, what was going to happen when she confronted Chris?

"I—I'm fine, Donna," she said at last, her mouth curving into an apologetic smile. "I didn't mean to snap at you. It's just . . . oh, jet lag, maybe. Or some kind of culture shock."

Donna accepted the apology and the explanation with an understanding nod. "Don't worry about it. You're entitled to a little temperament once in a while."

"Thanks. Is Chris around?"

"Is he ever!" Donna affirmed feelingly. "Honestly, I think the man sends out some kind of electronic signals. Five minutes after I got in this morning, the phone was ringing off the hook with calls from women who were just dying to tell him how glad they were he's finally back." She grimaced. "You'd think he'd been away for a year, not a week."

"It must be nice to be wanted," Allie said dryly.

"Oh, he's wanted, all right. Which means he gets everything *he* wants, just the way he wants it: free, fast, and no strings attached."

Allie cleared her throat. "Just where is Mr. Popularity at the moment?" she inquired sweetly.

"His office." Donna jabbed her thumb in the appropriate direction.

"Thanks."

The door to Chris's office was closed. Allie stood before it for several seconds, then knocked twice.

"Yeah?" Chris called.

"It's Allie."

"Come in. It's not locked."

Allie squared her shoulders, lifted her chin, and entered.

Chris's office was a jumble of controlled clutter. One full wall was devoted to a high-tech video system, complete with three playback machines and a custom-designed tape storage rack. The one opposite it was haphazardly hung with such items as a dart board, several Ansel Adams photographs, a vividly painted Chinese dragon kite, and a garishly colored poster for the movie *The Brain That Wouldn't Die*.

Most of the furniture was sleek, modern, and ex-

pensive. The one exception was the battered desk
Chris worked at. It had belonged to his grandfather—
the same one who had willed Chris the Rolex watch
he always wore.

Chris was at his desk, apparently going through a
backlog of correspondence. He was wearing jeans and
a partially unbuttoned blue work shirt. His dark-brown
hair was distinctly tousled.

As Donna had said, he looked gorgeous.

Allie felt her heart start to pound. God, was just
seeing him going to affect her like this? Any moment
now, for all her determination, she was going to lose
what small amount of self-control she had and—

"You're late," he told her without preamble.

His tone stopped her cold. She glanced at her watch.
She was running a bit behind schedule, but it was
unlike Chris to bring it up.

"Sorry," she said with a trace of uncertainty. "You
know how it is, the first day back."

"The point is, we *are* back. And part of your job
is to be here on time. Unless you think something's
happened to change that?"

Allie's hands clenched into fists. She'd heard Chris
use that same cool, cutting inflection once before on
a model who had tried to presume on her personal
relationship with him during a professional situation.
Having him turn it on her was like having him slam
a door in her face.

She took a steadying breath, forcing herself to relax
her fingers. All right. He'd drawn the line. She had
no intention of stepping over it.

"Allie?" There was still an edge in his voice.

"I apologize for being late," she returned.

He nodded. Something odd—could it be relief?—
flickered in the depths of his green eyes. "Fine. Now,
did you want something?"

She hesitated for a moment, wondering if this was

the time to approach him. But if not now, when? For the sake of her sanity, she needed her questions answered. She, too, needed to draw a few lines.

Slowly, Allie unzipped her woven leather shoulderbag and brought out the small box she'd found amid her things the night before. Walking forward, she placed it on Chris's desk. After a moment, she lifted the top, revealing the bracelet.

"I want to talk about this," she said simply.

She'd thought long and hard about the piece of jewelry during the night, turning it round and round in her fingers as she turned an endless and unanswerable chain of questions round and round in her mind. She'd asked herself *why*, over and over again; now she had to ask him.

"What's to talk about?" Chris picked up a pencil, drummed the eraser end on the desktop for a few seconds, then tossed it back down. He did not make a move to touch the bracelet.

"I need to know what it's supposed to mean." By the time she realized the admission implicit in her use of the words *I need*, it was too late to rephrase.

"Mean? It's a present, Allie. I saw you looking at it in that jeweler's shop and I got it for you. What's wrong? Don't you like it?"

"Of course I like it!" she answered instantly, responding to the challenge she heard threading through his question. "It's beautiful," she went on more moderately. "But—"

"But what? Did I leave the price tag on or something?"

Allie grimaced, unpleasantly aware of the fact that she was no longer in control of the conversation, if she ever had been to begin with. "No, you didn't."

"Then why the third degree? I've given you presents before, haven't I?"

"Oh, right!" she flared. "You've given me a book

of McDonald's gift certificates, season tickets to the Knicks, and an electric popcorn maker that you borrowed six months ago and never returned! This is *different*, Chris."

"How is it different?"

The same way you and I are different, she thought. I can't explain it, but I can feel it . . . and I don't think I like it.

"It just is!" she said, frustrated by her inability to find the right words and his stubborn refusal to give her the slightest bit of help.

"Allie . . ." He sounded so patient, so reasonable. Her temper broke.

"Look!" she burst out. "Just what is the bracelet? Some kind of 'Thanks for the fling' thing? Because, if it is—"

Chris rose, his eyes brilliant with undisguised anger. "What the hell kind of question is that?" he demanded.

Instinctively, Allie took a step back. When she realized what she'd done, she forced herself to stop retreating. "It's a perfectly logical question," she maintained hardily.

"Logical?" he spat out the word contemptuously. "You call it logical to insinuate that I'm trying to pay you off for going to bed with me?"

"Chris!"

"Maybe you'd like to accuse me of wanting to salve a guilty conscience, too?"

"No, I—"

"Or how about suggesting now that I've had my four days of fun with you, I'm attempting to bribe you to get out of my life?" he went on savagely.

"What am I supposed to think?" she threw at him, her wide brown eyes blazing with anger and confused hurt. A tiny part of her brain told her that neither one of them was behaving very rationally at the moment.

Chris swore. "How about thinking that I wanted to do something nice for you? How about thinking that I wanted to give you a surprise?"

"Well, you certainly surprised me!"

They glared at each other for several seconds. Allie realized she was trembling.

Chris took a deep, shuddery breath and expelled it slowly. He ran a hand back through his hair. The fingers of his other hand clenched into a white-knuckled fist and then relaxed.

"Allie..." he began. "Allie, I'm sorry. I didn't mean...I wasn't trying to..." He shook his head, his expression mirroring her own miserably mixed-up feelings.

Allie sighed, the anger going out of her. "I'm sorry, too, Chris," she murmured after a moment, making a palms-up gesture. "It's just that when I found the bracelet in my suitcase last night after what had happened between us, I thought...I don't know what I thought! But a present like that bracelet is so...special." She struggled to organize her jumbled thoughts. "Before we—you and I—before Antigua...Oh, God, Chris, I don't want what happened to change us!" she said with desperate sincerity. "That first morning after we made love, we talked about trying to work through whatever was b-bothering us. We also talked about going back—"

"—to the way things were," he completed. He closed his eyes for a moment, but not before she glimpsed a strange and disturbing expression flickering in their jade depths. When he looked at her again, the expression was gone. "Look, Allie, I don't want what happened to change us, either," he told her gently, coming out from behind the desk. "Believe me."

He moved to within touching distance of her. She was appalled—but not surprised—by the flutter of excitement his proximity stirred in her.

"Believe me," he repeated.

I believe you, she answered silently. I have to believe you.

She moistened her lips. "You think Antigua was a mistake, don't you?" she asked at last, repeating the question she'd put to him the morning she'd woken up in his bed for the first time. Her voice was remarkably steady.

His face tightened. "No," he said after an awful pause. "It wasn't a mistake—unless we turn it into one."

Which is exactly what will happen if you try to play the femme fatale, Allie told herself. Antigua is over! Grow up! Are you going to throw away two years of friendship because of four days?

"Do you think it was a mistake?" he questioned softly, his eyes fixed on her face. She read a strange mixture of yearning and determination in his expression. He lifted one hand as though reaching out to touch her cheek, but aborted the gesture with a quick clenching of his fingers. His hand dropped.

"How could anything that felt so good be a mistake?" she replied.

A sudden glint in his eyes told her he recognized the phrase. She got the peculiar feeling that it didn't please him, but he didn't pursue the issue.

"Will you keep the bracelet?" he asked after a moment, glancing back at his desk. "It's just a present, Allie. No strings attached. No hidden meanings."

If only there were strings!

"I'll keep it," she said, her tone as even as his. "It's beautiful, Chris. Thank you."

"You're welcome." He smiled tentatively. "Friends?"

She gave a little chuckle. "Do I have a choice?"

she retorted with a pinch of her usual sassiness.

The smile became a grin. "Nope."

"Friends, then. But only if you promise to give me back my popcorn popper."

"You've got it." Leaning forward, he dropped a chaste, "friendly" kiss on her nose. Before Allie had a chance to react, the door to Chris's office opened and Donna popped her head in.

"Oops," she said unrepentantly as Allie and Chris turned to look at her. "It got so quiet in here after all the yelling, I thought maybe you two had killed each other or something."

Chris moved away from Allie and back to his desk. With admirable nonchalance, he picked up the box with the bracelet. "No such luck, Donna," he said easily, extending the package to Allie. She took it with a wordless nod, not daring to meet his—or Donna's—eyes.

"Luck?" Donna snorted. "Do you have any idea how much extra work I'd have to do if I'd come in here and found you dead on the floor?"

"No. And I'm really not up to hearing the gory details at the moment."

"Actually, you getting murdered might lighten my load a little," the receptionist mused aloud. "But as for Allie—well, everybody knows she runs this place. Without her..."

Chris laughed, shaking his head. Although Allie didn't appreciate Donna's interruption, she was touched by the unsolicited testimonial. She wondered how much of her quarrel with Chris the receptionist had heard.

"You don't have to defend Allie to me, Donna," Chris said. "I know how important she is. Now, did you have a real reason for barging in here?"

Donna shot Allie a smile of female solidarity, and Allie had to smile back.

"Is there a problem, Donna?" she asked.

"Could be," the receptionist said, nodding. "I've got three charter members of the Chris Cooper fan club on hold and none of them will hang up until the boss talks to them."

"I'm beginning to see how Chris's murder might lighten your workload," Allie declared. She waggled her fingers at Chris. "Well, back to the way things used to be. I expect you to have my popcorn popper back to me by the end of the week, Chris," she added breezily. And with a provocative toss of her head, she exited his office.

Chapter

6

ALTHOUGH ALLIE HAD never considered herself much of an actress, she decided that her performance over the next week and a half rated at least an Academy Award nomination. There were moments when she even came close to convincing herself that what she felt for Chris was friendship.

Of course, coming close to convincing herself was not the same as actually doing it, but at least she managed to put up a good front.

As she had expected, word of her and Chris's little holiday had gone out over the industry grapevine long before they returned from Antigua. She dealt with the predictable knowing grins and envious comments with casual humor.

What she had not expected was the reaction she

got from the Strictly Commercial staff. After her paranoia of the first few days, she was surprised and oddly irked to discover that most of them simply assumed the time in Antigua had been nothing more than a long, buddy-buddy interlude. While Allie appreciated not having to cope with office gossip and speculation, she found herself perversely irritated that no one who really knew her seemed to think she was capable of carrying on a passionate liaison.

On the surface, she and Chris reverted to the relationship they had built up over the last two years. They resumed their on-the-job bickering matches as a matter of course and continued to meet for their customary after-hours tennis matches. Their instinctive attunement seemed as sensitive as ever. It was almost as though nothing had happened during those four days in the Caribbean, and Allie told herself she was glad.

But she was not glad when Chris, in typical fashion, turned up at her apartment the Saturday evening following their return from the island. He was laden with her popcorn popper, a grocery bag full of expensive goodies, and a copy of the latest *TV Guide*. After cheerfully dismissing her protests that she'd been about to wash her hair and go to bed early, he invited himself in for what he dramatically promised was going to be a "night to remember."

"Chris, I'll be perfectly honest with you," she said several hours later, washing down a handful of freshly popped corn with a mouthful of icy root beer. She'd been wearing nothing but her robe when he barged in earlier. Deciding that discretion was most definitely the better part of valor, she had changed into jeans and an oxford cloth shirt after it became clear that he was determined to settle in for the evening. "I don't think I can take another movie like *Attack of the Mushroom People*."

Chris grinned at her. "There are no other movies like *Attack of the Mushroom People*," he informed her. "Incidentally, I wish you'd refer to it by its proper title: *Matango, the Fungus of Terror*."

Allie rolled her eyes. They were sitting companionably in the living room of her one-bedroom apartment. He was comfortably sprawled on her couch, propped up by about half a dozen brightly colored throw pillows. She was curled up in the chintz-covered overstuffed chair that was one of the few items of furniture she'd salvaged from her marriage. Her nineteen-inch color television was carefully positioned between them for maximum viewing pleasure. Chris, naturally, had supervised the placement shortly after his unheralded arrival.

"Whatever you say," she replied. "But it beats me how a person of your alleged sophistication can wallow in this Grade-Z sci-fi stuff."

"This from a woman who owns a complete set of Dr. Seuss picture books?"

She grimaced. He knew her too well. "In any case, I really don't think I'm going to make it through the second part of this double feature." She glanced at her watch and stifled a yawn. "It's nearly one o'clock."

"Allie, you owe it to yourself to see *Plan Nine from Outer Space*."

"Why?"

"Because it's probably the worst movie ever made. You'll get a big kick out of it."

"I find it difficult to believe that there could be a worse movie than *Attack of the*—excuse me, *Mandingo, the Fungus of Terror*."

"*Matango*, Allie, *Matango!*"

"Whomever—or whatever. Just what is the big attraction of *Plan Nine?*"

"Do you like Bela Lugosi?"

"Is *he* in this picture?"

"Sort of. He, ah, died in the middle of filming."

Allie swirled her soda around in her glass, rattling the ice. She drank another mouthful. "Are you trying to tell me you want me to watch a movie with a dead person in it?" she inquired with distaste.

"No, of course not. What happened was, the director—the legendary Edward D. Wood, by the way—used the footage he'd shot of Lugosi, then had a double do the rest." He looked at her expectantly, his green eyes brilliant with mischief. For a moment, the vibrancy in his expression took Allie's breath away. She found his intensity and his enthusiasm—even when it came to something as ridiculously absurd as this—potently attractive.

Given her own affection for the ludicrous and offbeat, his affection for truly bad movies was especially appealing. Chris had occasionally regaled her with trivia about his favorite film fiascos, leaving her weak with disbelieving laughter over tales of idiotic ineptitude. Allie wondered suddenly if Chris had ever discussed his fondness for celluloid disasters with any of his other women. The possibility bothered her, as did the fact that she had forgotten that she was *not* one of his women—at least, not anymore.

"Aren't you going to ask who doubled for Lugosi?" Chris asked, intruding on her thoughts.

Allie looked at him. "No," she said.

"Al-lie," he complained. "Come on."

"Okay, okay," she gave in obediently, fighting down a giggle as she deliberately turned her mind from its troubling reflections. Chris was acting the same way her brothers used to act when they'd had secrets they wanted her to worm out of them. She put on an expression of wide-eyed curiosity. "Who did they get to double for the dead Mr. Lugosi?"

"You aren't treating this issue with the respect it deserves, you know." He chuckled, shaking his head.

"On the contrary. I'm treating it *just* the way it deserves to be treated." She tilted her head. "So? Are you going to answer my question or do I have to guess?"

"The double was an unemployed chiropractor."

"Darn! That was going to be my first guess."

"You're really a pain sometimes, do you know that?"

"If you say so. Now, tell me more about this unemployed chiropractor."

"Well, to begin with, he was about a foot taller than Lugosi and had blondish, not dark, hair."

"Ah."

"He also looked nothing like Bela."

"I see."

"But Edward Wood came up with a plan."

"Somehow, I thought he might." Absently, she leaned over and reached into the bowl of popcorn. Instead of grabbing a handful of the buttery treat, her fingers collided with his. She felt a kind of electric shock at the contact.

"Hey," she started to joke, trying to cover her reaction. "Don't hog all the pop . . . corn." Her voice trailed off as their eyes met. What she thought she saw in the depths of his green gaze made her mouth go dry. "C-Chris?" she faltered.

He withdrew his hand from the bowl. Looking away for a moment, he rubbed his greasy fingers carelessly against his thigh. "Sorry," he muttered. He shifted his position once or twice before he looked back at her. "I'll make more if you want."

"No, that's okay." She took a sip of root beer. "You, uh, were telling me about Edward Wood's plan?"

He relaxed slightly. "Right. Wood simply told the double to wear a black cape—like Lugosi—and to hold it in front of his face at all times. Brilliant, hmm?"

Allie let her mouth drop open. "You actually expect me to stay up and watch this thing?" she demanded.

He gave her a crooked smile. "You'll love it."

While she didn't precisely love the movie, it did have a wackily compelling quality. Still, as fascinating as she found the sight of flying hubcaps (meant to be the invading aliens' spaceships) and a female character called Vampira, Allie found her eyelids growing heavier and heavier with each passing commercial.

She only partially woke up when Chris lifted her gently out of her chair and began carrying her toward her bedroom.

"Adam?" she murmured sleepily, uncertainly. Her mind was foggy with confusion and flickering images of mushroom-covered monsters.

"Chris," he corrected.

"Oh," she sighed, strangely reassured. She nuzzled her face against his shoulder, breathing in his scent. She was dreamily aware of the warmth and strength of his body . . . and of the shudder that ran through him as her lips touched the bare skin of his neck. How could I have thought it was Adam? she wondered. This is Chris . . .

She made a little sound, low in her throat.

Tired. She was very tired. She hadn't been sleeping very well.

"It's okay, Allie," Chris told her softly. "I'm just putting you to bed."

Her mouth curled into a delicious, crooked smile. "Good idea . . . mmm . . ."

He laid her down on the bed, spreading her hair out over the pillow with gentle fingers. He didn't bother to turn on the overhead light, so even if she had opened her eyes, she wouldn't have been able to read his expression. With the blissful oblivion of sleep beckoning, Allie barely felt him slip off her sneakers and carefully undo the top buttons of her shirt.

A tiny part of her mind did register the fleeting kiss he dropped on her faintly parted lips.

Chris. Always Chris. Never Adam.

"You can stay," she mumbled.

"No, I can't," he returned. "Good night, Brown Eyes."

She awoke the next morning alone and frustrated. She spent the rest of the weekend in the same state.

She didn't remember exactly what had happened in the wee hours of Saturday night, but she did remember asking Chris to stay. She also remembered his refusal. Her body ached with the memory of it. She felt a deepening sexual yearning and a kind of miserable inadequacy each time she thought about it.

The week that followed was a busy one at Strictly Commercial. It was a busy one *outside* Strictly Commercial, too, at least as far as Chris was concerned. If there had been any truth to Parrish's observation that Chris had slowed the pace of his social life before the trip to Antigua, there was certainly none of it afterward. Allie told herself over and over again that she wasn't jealous of the seemingly endless string of stunning women who trailed after him, but she couldn't help wanting to scream "What about me?" every once in a while.

Why me?! was what she came very close to screaming the following Friday as she struggled to survive a location shoot for a men's deodorant commercial.

The day started out with the news that Strictly Commercial's ace lighting director had hurt his back falling over his son's skateboard and was going to be out of commission for at least two weeks. It went downhill from there.

Blown fuses. A breakdown in the camera crew's van. A misplaced lens. A hairdresser with a raging case of hay fever. An agency account executive with a penchant for making unneeded and unwanted suggestions at precisely the wrong moment. Those were just a few of the things Allie had to cope with.

In addition to trying to handle these problems, she also had to contend with a sudden upsurge of tension between herself and Chris. Because it was unseasonably hot, and because the shoot was outdoors at a private tennis club, Allie had dressed in white shorts and a sleeveless knit tank top. Chris had reacted to the outfit as though she'd decided to parade down Fifth Avenue in a see-through bikini. While she managed to refrain from telling him what she thought about his absurdly puritanical attitude, she could not help muttering a few remarks about hypocrisy when, after an hour in the sun, Chris nonchalantly stripped down to nothing but his skin-tight jeans.

The biggest headache of all, however, was the star of the commercial: a world-class tennis champion with an oversized male ego and a pair of roaming hands. Although Allie did her best to keep her distance from him, the requirements of her job made that very difficult. To make matters even worse, the man seemed to mistake her polite rebuffs for coyness. The second time she removed his palm from her rear end, he actually had the gall to leer, wink, and mutter something about "the thrill of the chase."

Parrish Williams was the makeup artist for the commercial and, to Allie's eternal gratitude, he did his best to run a bit of interference for her. A vanity-ridden fifty-year-old movie queen trying to pass for thirty wouldn't have gotten as many touch-ups as Parrish gave the tennis star.

"Look, just lay off me, will you?" the former Wimbledon champion finally burst out after Parrish had skillfully deflected yet another of his grabs for some portion of Allie's anatomy. "Leave me alone!"

Parrish arched his brows and cocked his head. He fixed the outraged jock with a gimlet-eyed stare. "I'm only trying to do my job," he declared huffily, then turned to Allie. "Isn't that right, Allie darling? I'm only doing my job!"

"Um, you *do* need a little something on your face," Allie told her admirer, confirming Parrish's words with a nod. In repayment for this good deed, she vowed that she'd let Parrish cut her hair or paint her green or anything else he wanted.

"Oh, yeah?" the tennis star challenged, looking slightly offended.

Allie nodded again, not trusting herself to answer. Yeah, she thought wrathfully. And I'd like to be the one to give you the little something for your face, too: right in the nose!

"Well, I don't like guys with powder puffs flitting around me," the athlete said in a drawling, unpleasant tone. "Especially not when they're getting in the way of something I want."

The slur against Parrish, as well as the salaciousness of the last remark, made Allie put her chin up.

Okay, you jerky jock—

Before she could speak aloud, a firm and cautioning hand came down on her shoulder.

"I'll take care of this, Allie," Chris said coolly.

The tennis star blinked and began to look distinctly uncomfortable. "Hey, now, look—" he started, using the same voice Allie had heard him use when complaining about a referee's call during a televised match.

"No, *you* look," Chris cut him off, his tone and bearing dangerously controlled. Parrish had edged back, neatly disengaging himself from the scene yet watching what was happening with undisguised fascination. "You're here to pitch deodorant, not to paw my producer. If you so much as lay another finger on her, I will ram your personally endorsed tennis racquet and a couple of your personally endorsed tennis balls down your throat."

"Chris!" Allie shrieked, not quite able to believe what she'd just heard.

He ignored her, staring levelly at the champion, who looked peculiarly like the proverbial little boy caught with his hand in the cookie jar.

"Do you understand?" Chris asked flatly, biting off each syllable.

The tennis star's eyes darted back and forth between Allie and Chris for several seconds. She could practically see his mind working. She wondered if he was on the verge of one of his fabled temper tantrums.

"She didn't seem to mind," he said to Chris at last, putting forward this patent falsehood in a surprisingly mild voice. Allie gritted her teeth, and Chris squeezed her shoulder warningly.

"Maybe not," he said. "But *I* did."

For a moment, Allie thought she might choke. But to her appalled astonishment, the other man started to chuckle. He gave Chris what could only be described as a locker-room grin of macho understanding. "Oh, I get it," he drawled with a knowing wink. "Hey, man, I didn't realize I was poaching on private property—"

"No, *man,* you still don't get it," Chris interrupted. "The lady is nobody's property—least of all, mine."

"Then what's the problem?"

"The problem is that you're keeping my producer

from doing her job. Now, I want you to forget about the foreplay and concentrate on your forehand so we can get this damned commercial shot. Is that understood?"

There was a short, tense pause. For one horrible moment, Allie thought the face-off might degenerate into something much worse. Then, to her surprise, the bullying force went out of the athlete and he deflated like a balloon.

"Yeah, it's understood," he said. "Let me get warmed up again, and we can do the service sequence." He glanced resignedly at Parrish. "If you've got to put more of your goop on my face, you might as well come along and do it now."

The tennis champion loped off, trailed by the smugly smiling makeup artist. They were barely out of earshot when Allie whirled on Chris, brown eyes blazing.

"Damn you, Chris," she hissed, struggling to keep from shouting. She was bitterly aware that everyone on the crew had been watching—and listening to—them for the past five minutes. "How could you do something like that?"

"Something like what?" he challenged scathingly. "What the hell is the matter with you, Allie? Were you getting some kind of kick out of having Mr. Foot Fault cop a feel every ten seconds?"

"I was handling it!"

"Oh, right, you were handling it," he sneered sarcastically. "If Parrish hadn't been sticking makeup sponges into the guy's face and dancing around him like Rudolph Nureyev, you would have been in serious trouble. Not that you weren't asking—"

"What?" This time she didn't even try to keep her voice down.

His eyes raked her slender figure. "Just look at you! You read enough sports columns to know our anti-perspirant pitchman is a spoiled brat on the court and a legend in his own mind as a womanizer off it. Couldn't you have worn something a little less provocative today?"

"Like what? A pup tent?"

"How about a bra?"

"I *am* wearing a bra!"

"Well, you couldn't prove it by me," he retorted.

"I wasn't aware I had to prove anything to anybody," she told him through gritted teeth. "Least of all, you."

For a split second, he seemed on the verge of really losing his temper. Then he visibly reined himself in and shook his head. "Forget it. Just forget it. We've got a commercial to shoot."

With that, he turned on his heel and stalked back to his camera setup.

You, Allie thought, staring after him with murder in her eyes, are the only thing around here likely to get shot today.

"Parrish, why did you bring me here?" she inquired wearily a number of hours later. They were sitting in a rather preciously decorated wine bar on the Upper East Side. Allie's casual outfit had not merited so much as a second glance; in fact, she looked positively overdressed compared to most of the other patrons.

"I brought you here because I need a drink. And if I need one, you probably need six or seven." He nodded at the glass that had been set in front of her. "Believe me, you'll feel much better once you have one of those."

"What is it?" she asked without much enthusiasm.

"It's a champagne cocktail. A little of this, a little of that, and plenty of the bubbly."

"My brothers told me never to drink anything that

has more than three ingredients."

"Down the hatch, darling," Parrish advised, taking a sip of his own drink. Allie followed suit after a moment. Actually, the concoction tasted quite good. If she hadn't been in such a foul mood, she might have enjoyed it.

By some miracle, they'd finished their shoot without any further problems after her blow up with Chris. The tennis star had behaved himself impeccably and the crew had performed with unusual inspiration. Of course, Chris had barely spoken to her and she'd developed a pounding headache from glaring at him, but that was only to be expected.

"I'd like to kill him," she said aloud, fingering the stem of her glass with a scowl.

"Who? Attila the Tennis Bum?"

She shook her head. "Do you know, I actually admired him until today? I felt sorry he couldn't play in this year's U.S. Open because of his tendonitis. But now—yechh!"

"Life is full of little disillusionments," Parrish observed. "But who is it you'd like to kill?"

"Chris!"

"Ah."

"Did you hear him today?"

"Umm. I was quite impressed, I must say. Especially with the part about ramming the racquet down our star's throat. I thought the 'personally endorsed' bit was really effective."

Allie looked up from her drink. "You are an extremely sick person, Parrish Williams," she told him.

"So my ex-therapist used to say," he returned pleasantly.

"What would make Chris act like that?" she demanded.

Parrish studied her for several seconds. "Well, offhand, I can only think of two explanations: one, he's lost his mind; or two, he's so jealous he can't see straight—which, come to think of it, is essentially the same thing as losing his mind."

Allie choked on her drink, nearly spitting a mouthful of it across the table. She had to struggle to catch her breath. "Jealous?" she croaked. "Why should he be—"

"Allie, *please*. I realize you're a little warped in a few places, but even you can't be that naïve." He paused. "I take it I was wrong in not assuming the worst about those couple of days you and Chris spent in Antigua? Martine swore to me that nothing was going on between you two while she was there."

"Nothing was."

"But?" he prompted.

Allie put one elbow on the table and rested her forehead in her hand. "Chris and I had a ... fling," she confessed finally. "After Martine left."

"Well, good for you."

"Parrish!" she groaned, looking over at him despairingly.

"It wasn't good for you?" He frowned concernedly.

Allie went bright red. "Yes, it was good for me," she admitted. "I don't know how good it was for Chris, though," she added, not really meaning to say the words aloud.

Parrish tapped his fingers against his mouth, his button-black eyes thoughtful. "I see," he commented without elaboration. Allie had the crazy notion that somehow he *did* see. "Sweetie, you haven't got a case of 'Does he still respect me?' do you? I mean, it's not as though you and Chris had a one-night stand, is it?"

"It was a four-night stand, actually," she said.

"I beg your pardon?"

Allie sighed. For all his posturing, she knew that Parrish's interest was motivated by genuine feelings of affection. Behind his bitchy, brittle comments, there was a firm and reliable core of caring and common sense.

Slowly, then with increasing fluency, she told him what had happened on Antigua. Parrish nodded encouragingly through her recitation, his expression full of sympathetic understanding.

"And so," Allie concluded, "we came back to New York."

"Having had your fling."

"Right. And now we're just friends again."

"I see. What happened today at the shoot was 'just friendship'?"

"I don't *know* what happened at today's shoot," she admitted, unconsciously toying with the gold, opal, and coral braclet that circled her left wrist. She'd put it on after her confrontation with Chris at the office that first day back from Antigua and, without seriously considering the implications, had gotten into the habit of wearing it most of the time since.

"Neither do I," Parrish confessed wryly.

"I mean, why in heaven's name did he carry on about my clothes that way? Did you think there was anything indecent about the way I looked?" She didn't give him a chance to answer. "After all, *he* was strutting around like something out of a beefcake calendar in those jeans of his! If you want to talk about indecent—"

"Never mind that," Parrish cut in smoothly. "So you two aren't seeing each other?"

"Oh, we're seeing each other. At work. After work to play tennis. And he came over to my apartment last weekend to watch *Attack of the Mushroom People*."

"You mean *Matango, the Fungus of Terror*."

"Oh, God, not you, too."

"Who do you think turned Chris on to bad movies?"

Allie shook her head. "I can't take it anymore. I give up."

"Not yet, please. But, I repeat, you're not seeing each other?"

"Not the way you mean, no." She grimaced. "You heard what Chris said: I'm nobody's property, least of all his."

"Hmm."

"But don't worry," she went on, her voice a little ragged. "He's not suffering from sexual frustration. He's had women parading in and out of Strictly Commercial ever since we got back from the Caribbean. I'm thinking about having a conveyor belt installed."

"Well, there is a certain amount of safety in numbers," Parrish observed obliquely, swirling his drink.

"What?"

"Nothing, nothing. Maybe you should buy him one of those take-a-number things like they have in bakeries."

Allie managed a weak smile. "Frankly, I don't know how he keeps track of them. They look so disgustingly similar: gorgeous, gorgeous, and more gorgeous."

"Maybe he can't, and that's why he calls them all Babe or Honey."

Allie's smile changed into a frown. "Maybe," she agreed. Now that she considered it, she realized that Chris had never used any of the usual endearments with her. Even when they'd made love . . .

Parrish reached over and gently patted her hand. "It's going to be okay," he encouraged her.

She looked at him. "I don't think so," she said sadly. I'm in love with Chris, she thought, but he's not in love with me. Even if he was jealous today, jealousy isn't love.

"Well, at least try to tell yourself that things can't get any worse," the makeup man suggested bracingly.

Parrish was wrong. Things could get worse, and they did. Three days later, Adam Phipps—Allie's ex-husband—showed up at Strictly Commercial.

Chapter

7

"ARE YOU ALL RIGHT, Allie?" Chris asked softly, his expression holding equal parts of grimness and concern. They were standing outside the conference room at Strictly Commercial. Adam and his colleague had been shepherded inside by Donna. Chris had fabricated some convincing excuse to allow him a moment alone with Allie before they, too, went into the meeting.

"Fine," she said, wondering if she looked as pale as she felt. Seeing Adam again had been such a shock! And coming on top of the nerve storms of the previous two weeks . . .

"He really gets to you, doesn't he?" Chris's voice was taut.

Allie shot him a reproachful look, stung by what

she took to be an accusing undertone in the question. "I didn't expect to see him," she answered stiffly. "I had no idea he'd even changed jobs." Her brows drew together in a moment of pained conjecture. "You didn't know, did you?"

The flash of temper she saw in his eyes was so intense that she instinctively looked away. Her emotions were very raw at the moment, and she knew she wasn't prepared to cope with even the mildest confrontation with Chris.

He caught her chin and forced her to face him. "No, damn it, I didn't know. I had no idea Ed Dillon was getting kicked upstairs and they were bringing in a new head of the advertising department at FideliCo. Do you honestly think I would have let you walk into this unprepared if I'd realized who was going to be involved?" He let go of her. *"Do you?"*

His touch had sent a tremor of reaction running through her. The open-necked collar of her turquoise wrap dress revealed the wildly pounding pulse in the hollow of her throat.

Allie shook her head, ashamed of her suspicions and desperately afraid of what he must be reading in her face.

"I'm—I'm sorry," she said. "No, of course I don't think that." Her voice was slightly unsteady. Unable to help herself, she reached out and touched his arm. He'd held her, made love to her, carried her to bed. And now...

She chopped off that thought with a silent moan of despair. "I don't think that," she repeated. "It's just that, after n-nearly two years..." She couldn't explain. "I'm all right. I'm okay. Let's go."

Without giving him a chance to say anything more, she took a deep breath and marched into the conference room.

Allie got through the meeting without faltering, discharging her responsibilities with a single-minded efficiency. She had too much pride to do anything else. Fortunately, she'd worked on another series of FideliCo commercials the year before, and she understood the conservative, straightforward approach the company favored. Except for the two or three times she glanced up from her notes and found Adam watching her with a look of intrigued curiosity, his behavior during the session was pleasant and professional. Her biggest problem during the meeting was her acute awareness of Chris.

I'm sitting in a room with the only two men in the world I've ever gone to bed with, she thought. One is a man I lived with for five years; the other is someone I had a four-day fling with. I can barely remember those five years. But those four days...

Those four days had changed her life; she realized that. No matter what happened, the Allie Douglas who went to Antigua was not the same one who came back. The latter woman knew she'd found the man she could love for the rest of her life. That same woman also knew she couldn't have him—at least not as her lover.

But as her friend?

Adam put a brief, restraining hand on her arm after the discussion broke up and Chris and Ed Dillon left the conference room. Steeling herself to face whatever was coming, Allie turned and looked at him, her expression controlled.

"How are you, Adam?" she asked, determined to take the initiative. Oddly, now that the shock of seeing him had subsided, she was surprised to discover how little effect he really had on her.

"I'm fine, Allison," Adam replied. He was one of the few people who'd ever called her by her given name. While she'd liked it at first, she'd come to resent it, viewing his rejection of her nickname as a rejection of her real self. "It was quite a surprise seeing you here. An unexpected pleasure."

Her eyes widened. This was not what she'd anticipated. "It was a surprise for me, too," she said carefully.

"You look lovely."

"Thank you," she responded, puzzled but polite. She supposed she did look reasonably attractive; she was wearing one of her best "client" outfits, after all. But *lovely?* "It's kind of you to say that. But I'm still the same old Allie."

Adam shook his head. He was about two inches taller than she was and of a medium build. His hair was brown and his eyes were hazel. He was attractive in a successful-executive kind of way, but he had very little of Chris's coiled-spring energy or sexual magnetism. His clothes—a gray suit, white shirt, and burgundy tie—were well-tailored and in excellent taste, but they looked ordinary and almost stodgy compared with the quiet European elegance of Chris's discreetly expensive navy-blue suit.

"No, not the same. You've changed."

"I'm two years older and wiser than the last time you saw me," she returned lightly. "How's Bethany?"

It was a bitchy thing to ask, but she wanted to know. Bethany was the woman he had left her for.

Adam flushed. "It didn't work out. We—she broke off the engagement."

"Oh." Allie had done her hair in a chignon that morning, and she reached up to pat a few stray strands back into place. As she did so, she was conscious of the weight of Chris's bracelet moving on her wrist. She saw Adam register the distinctive piece of jewelry with a tightening of his lips. "I'm sorry."

He gave a sour little chuckle. "The Douglas brand of good sportsmanship?" he asked.

That tone, at least, was familiar. But it no longer had the power to hurt her.

"My father taught me to be a good loser," she said simply. He also taught me to fight like hell when I want something, she thought suddenly.

Adam made a small gesture of surrender. "I wasn't trying to bait you," he said sincerely. "I apologize for the way that came out. But seeing you has knocked me for a loop." He shifted and glanced around, and Allie could tell he was impressed by the sleek, sophisticated décor of the conference room. She'd come a long way from her gofer job in Chicago.

"You must be doing very well here," Adam said after a pause. "Ed was raving about you—not by name, of course—on the flight out. And Chris Cooper and Strictly Commercial have quite a reputation in the advertising field."

"I like what I'm doing," Allie said sincerely.

"It shows. Look, I'm going to be in town through the weekend. Do you suppose we could get together? For a drink, maybe—or dinner?"

"Well..." She hesitated, genuinely torn. She was human enough to be flattered by Adam's obviously positive reaction to her, but she wasn't sure she wanted to commit herself to seeing him again outside of a business situation.

"Why don't I call you around the middle of the week?" he suggested quickly. "I'm not trying to pressure you into anything, Allison," he continued. "But I would very much like to get together with you—for old times' sake, shall we say."

"All right," she agreed, relieved to have gained a little breathing space. "I'll talk to you later in the week, then, Adam."

"So, that was your ex," Chris said about fifteen minutes later. Adam and Ed Dillon had just been ushered out, and Chris had called Allie into his office on some clearly manufactured pretext.

"That was my ex," she agreed neutrally, feeling as though she was trying to tap dance on egg shells. She couldn't get a fix on Chris's mood, and that troubled her. They'd always been so open with each other—before Antigua, that is.

"He seemed glad to see you." He'd already shucked off his jacket, and now he pulled his tie loose with an irritated jerk.

"Umm."

Oh, Chris, she thought, what's happened to us? We haven't gone back to the way things used to be. We've gone from intimacy to estrangement.

Losing Adam hadn't been this bad. It had been hard, yes: she'd felt betrayed and her pride had been wounded, but she hadn't felt as though someone was slowly, inexorable cutting her heart in two. She hadn't felt that in losing Adam she was losing half of herself.

"Were you glad to see him?" Chris made an unnecessary adjustment of his cuffs. "For a couple of seconds there, I thought you were going to pass out."

"As I said before, I was surprised."

"Surprised. Right." He fiddled with some papers on his desk. Allie had never seen him so pointlessly restless. It made her uncomfortable to watch him. Somewhere in the back of her mind, a memory stirred: the memory of a jungle cat she'd seen in a cage at the zoo when she was a little girl. She had found the image troubling then; for reasons she couldn't quite name, she found it infinitely more distressing now.

"Chris—"

"He's going to be in town for a few days, you know," he went on casually, toying with another stack of papers.

What was he searching for? Did he *want* her to say

she was glad to see Adam again?

"I know," she answered evenly, trying to swallow the lump that had formed in her throat. "He wants to take me out for a drink . . . or dinner."

His dark head came up. "I see." Before he could elaborate, however, his interoffice line rang. He picked up the phone. "Yeah, what?" he demanded abruptly, then listened for several seconds. "Hold on," he said. "You've got a call on your line, Allie," he told her, covering the mouthpiece with his palm. "It's your brother J.J. Do you want it transferred in here?"

"No, thanks," she said quickly, grateful for an excuse to get away from him. "I'll go into my own office."

She dashed down the hallway to her modest work area and picked up the phone, her mind racing through the reasons J.J. might have called her at work.

"J.J.?" she said breathlessly into the receiver. "It's Allie. What's wrong?"

Her eldest brother's warmly familiar chuckle came over the line. "Nothing's wrong, Sis. I know I probably shouldn't have phoned you at the office, but I haven't heard from you in a while and it's just about impossible to get you at home. So, I thought I'd give you a quick buzz—you know, play big brother."

Allie sank into her chair. "J.J.—"

"Yeah, I know, I know. You're all grown up and don't need me checking on you. But never mind that. How are you, kid?"

"Fine," Allie replied automatically, then sighed. "Well, maybe not all that fine."

"What's the matter?" His voice lost the lighthearted quality she loved.

She hesitated, gnawing at her lower lip. There was no way she could tell him the whole story. "Adam showed up today." she said finally.

"Adam?"

"Yes, Adam. Adam Phipps, my ex-husband."

"Don't get cute. What the hell is he doing in New York?"

She explained the situation in a few sentences.

J.J. snorted. "I thought you sounded down when you answered."

"I'm not down!" she denied vehemently. "I was just a little surprised to see him, that's all."

"I'll bet."

Allie played with her gold-and-opal bracelet. "You know," she confided slowly, "it was strange seeing him again. I thought I'd feel more. But, well, I didn't feel much of anything beyond the surprise. Maybe a little regret. He seemed—I don't know—nice, I guess. Nicer than I remembered, really."

"Nice?" J.J.'s tone turned thunderous. "That son of a—"

"J.J.!" she cut in sharply. She'd forgotten the kind of grudge all three of her brothers harbored against Adam on her behalf.

"Did that creep bother you?"

"Of course not! Don't be silly."

"What does Chris say?"

Her heart skipped a few beats. "Chris? What does he have to do with this?"

"If Adam bothers you, he'll have a lot to do with it. He'll probably belt the guy."

"Are you crazy? Adam's a *client!*"

"So?"

"J.J., for heaven's sake! Chris would never—"

"Of course he would." J.J. laughed. "He's that kind of guy. If somebody was causing problems for you, he'd take care of it—same as Rick, Mark, or I would."

Allie grimaced, keenly sensitive to the irony of her brother's view of things.

"But how do you know that?" she persisted.
"You've only met him once—unless you've been
going behind my back?"

"Don't be paranoid, Allie. Nobody's been going
behind your back. I didn't need to meet Chris more
than once to figure out what he's like. Besides, Pop
met him last year, too, remember? And he liked him
a lot. In fact—"

Allie abruptly decided it was time to change the
topic. "How did we get off on the subject of Christian
Cooper?" she inquired irritably. She was spending
enough time working with Chris and thinking about
Chris—she didn't want to talk about him, too. She
especially didn't want to talk about him with an older
brother whose perceptiveness had caused her more
than a few acutely uncomfortable moments during her
childhood and adolescence.

"You were the one who—"

"Never mind. I don't want to talk about him—or
me, for that matter."

J.J. gave a theatrical sigh. "Do I get the feeling
I'm being told to butt out of something?"

"W-e-e-ll," she drew the word out.

"Say no more. I can take a hint. I realize that Mark,
Rick, and I—to say nothing of Pop—come on a little
strong sometimes. But we only do it because we love
you, Allie, and we don't want you to get hurt."

She smiled at the receiver, her eyes soft. "I know.
And I love you all, too. But I am twenty-seven and
I've been through a divorce and I can take care of
myself." She crossed her fingers in a childish gesture.
It was impossible to say whether she was doing so
for luck or to counteract the lie she was telling. "Now,
how are *you?*"

"Me? Never better."

"How's Introduction to Western Civilization?" J.J.

taught history at the University of Illinois.

"I've only had five students fall asleep so far."

"They'll wake up when you get to the sexy parts." They shared a laugh. "Look, J.J., I do appreciate your call."

"Hey, what's a brother for if not to bug his sister once in a while. Take care, okay?"

"You too," she said. "Bye." And smiling to herself, Allie hung up the phone.

Chris had departed for the day by the time Allie finally came out of her office. She didn't have to wonder how he spent his evening. He and his "blond beauty" date were written up in a newspaper gossip column the next morning.

"Burning the candle at both ends?" she twitted him that afternoon after watching him yawn his way through a staff meeting on the upcoming snack-food shoot. The tone she used was the same one she'd employed as a girl when teasing her brothers about their love lives. It was the same one she'd used in the past when teasing Chris about his.

This time, however, he did not respond with a quip or a joke, as usual.

"What's that supposed to mean?" he snapped, scrawling his signature on the bottom of a sheet of paper. He looked up at her, his green eyes full of wary challenge.

"Mean?" she echoed, taken aback by his reaction. "Nothing special. You and last night's lady friend made one of the columns this morning, that's all."

"I didn't know you were keeping such close tabs on me." His tone clearly indicated that he didn't like this idea.

Her brows came together. "I'm not," she denied. "I happened to see the item and I thought—"

"You thought you'd get in some little dig."

"No!" she said immediately, beginning to be as indignant as she was puzzled.

"You know, I don't like jealousy—"

"*Jealousy?!* Why should I be jealous of somebody who probably can't even remember what her real hair color is? Look, why are you being so touchy? I've kidded you about this kind of thing before—"

"*Before,*" he cut her off, stressing the word with brutal emphasis. "That's just the point."

Allie's eyes flashed with angry hurt. "Chris!"

"I've been doing my best to get things between us back to normal," he said, "trying to keep a lid on the speculation—"

"Like telling the Tennis King you had no claim on me?" she flared, fighting down the urge to pick something up and fling it at him. "I don't understand you anymore, Chris! You talk one way but you act another, and I keep getting caught in the middle. Just what do you want of me?"

He stared at her, his face a study in tension. The skin was taut over his cheekbones, and there were lines of strain around his mouth. He seemed to be fighting some desperate physical impulse. "I . . . want you . . . to leave me alone."

"You don't mean that," she said, shaken by his words and the desperate way he'd uttered them. Instinctively, she reached out to touch him. His body went rigid as he read her intention, and he warned her off with his eyes. "Chris, please . . ."

"Dammit, Allie! If you aren't going to help, will you at least get off my back?" he lashed out.

She said something that would have gotten her mouth washed out with soap when she was a child. "Well, excuse me! You know, one of these days, you're going to have to explain to me your ground rules for getting things between us 'back to normal.' That's assuming, of course, that you've figured the ground rules out!" She took a deep breath. "And as for my getting off your back—don't worry! I never thought that portion of your anatomy was particularly attractive anyway."

Allie didn't have to wonder about Chris's activities that night, either. While switching curiously through the late-night local news broadcasts in search of something less depressing than nonstop reports on fires, murders, and political squabbles, she saw a shot of him getting out of a limousine with the sultry brunette star of a New York–based soap opera.

Even without the gnawing ache of hurt and uncertainty eating away at her, Allie would not have classed Wednesday as one of her better days. By the time she finally arrived at the office—frazzled from having overslept and then been stuck in a broken-down subway car for thirty-five minutes—she'd begun to think the world was conspiring against her. A few needling comments from Chris and a testy phone conversation with one of their equipment suppliers about some shipping damages did nothing to change her opinion.

An apparently endless series of auditions for a baby-food commercial confirmed her assessment of the situation. But the coup de grace came when one of the infants decided to demonstrate his lack of enthusiasm for a bowl of pureed beets by dumping it all over her new white silk blouse.

After maturely résisting the impulse to retaliate by pouring a bowl of creamed spinach on the child's head, Allie tersely excused herself and retired to the bathroom to try to repair the damage. Chris barged into the lavatory about five minutes later.

She was bent over the sink, naked to the waist

except for a skimpy bra, furiously scrubbing at the brilliant red stain. At Chris's unannounced entrance she flushed and straightened up as though her spine had been replaced by a broomstick.

"What do you want?" she asked rudely, glaring at him.

He stood there for a moment, silent and unmoving. Then, slowly, his eyes ran down her body. His gaze was as tangible as a touch.

Allie's throat closed up and her stomach knotted. Acting on instinct, she clutched the now-sodden top to her chest like a shield. The ruined garment dripped liberally down her jeans and onto her shoes. She didn't know which she wanted to do more: cry, hit Chris with her shirt, or melt into his arms.

"Will you please get out of here?" she demanded through gritted teeth.

His eyes traveled back up her body, lingering on the soft swell of her breasts. The wet blouse didn't really offer much coverage; it was nearly transparent. She could feel her nipples contract into stiff, aching peaks in response to his searing scrutiny. Trembling, she held the soaking top even closer. Why didn't he say something?

His eyes came to rest on her hot-cheeked face. His stare was steady and disturbingly intense. He stood there, motionless, yet the air around him seemed to vibrate with his powerful maleness.

When he finally spoke, his voice was low and very controlled. "I thought you might be able to use this." he said, holding out a faded but serviceable sweat shirt Allie recognized as one of those he kept stashed in his office along with a cache of athletic gear.

After a short hesitation, she took the proffered garment with an ungracious nod. Chris's eyes had not wavered from her face since he'd completed that first assessing survey of her body. Frowning, Allie dropped her blouse into the sink. Turning her back to him for a moment, she pulled on the sweat shirt.

"My blouse is ruined, you know," she informed Chris tautly as her head emerged from the roomy garment. She tugged the sweat shirt down as she faced him again. Her hair, which had been pulled off her forehead with a large barrette, was streaming loose over her shoulders. She knew she must look like a pathetic ragamuffin.

"I would have thought you'd have more brains than to wear a white silk blouse on the day we were auditioning babies," he replied with maddening logic.

"You'd think I'd have more brains than to do a lot of things lately," she snapped, stung by his attitude.

It had been foolish to wear the blouse; she was perfectly aware of that. But she'd been so unsettled this morning that she had simply snatched up and put on the first thing that came to hand. Still, even given the inappropriateness of the garment, she thought he should at least have the decency to be a little sympathetic. After all, she'd nobly refrained from giggling the time an elephant had sprayed him with mud during a location shoot for a car commercial. And he'd looked a lot sillier coated with gooey brown earth than she had with beets on her blouse!

"You said it, Allie, I didn't," he returned. "Now, if you're done in here, you've got a phone call waiting. It's your ex-husband. Once you two get done plotting your reconciliation date or rendezvous or whatever, maybe we can get back to work, hmm?"

"Maybe," Allie said, lifting her chin. She swept her hair back behind her ears in a careless gesture. What difference did it make how she looked, anyway? Chances were, she'd end up getting thrown up on or wet on before the day's session was over.

Considering the way things were going, she'd probably be thrown up on *and* wet on!

Brushing past Chris, she stalked out of the bathroom, took her call, and agreed to have dinner with Adam on Friday night.

Chapter

8

AFTERWARD, ALLIE WAS never too certain about her reasons for accepting Adam's invitation. In fact, within moments of hanging up the phone, she was tempted to call him back and change her "yes" to a "no." If it hadn't been for Chris hovering within earshot, she might have done just that.

She was honest enough with herself to admit that part of her motivation for agreeing to go out with Adam stemmed from her jealous reaction to Chris's stepped-up social schedule since their return from Antigua. It was not something she was particularly proud of, but it was a fact.

There was also an element of curiosity in her decision. She had, after all, been married to Adam for five years, and she had loved him—or at least she'd

129

thought she did. Allie wondered if any of her old feelings for him were lying dormant, or whether they were all well and truly dead. A date would give her a chance to test herself and to see how much Adam had changed in the past two years, if at all.

Finally, she'd accepted his invitation because she was flattered by it. For all his faults, Adam had never been a very good dissembler, and she knew he hadn't been faking the look of astonished admiration in his eyes at his first glimpse of her in two years. She'd impressed her ex-husband, perhaps even attracted him. That knowledge was balm to her battered ego.

Strangely—disappointingly, a tiny part of her mind admitted with ruthless frankness—Chris took the news that she was going out with Adam without any visible reaction. He simply nodded and quietly announced it was time to get back to work. His mood for the rest of the day, and the day after that, was friendly but oddly aloof. He treated Allie with a restrained, hands-off consideration that she found almost more unnerving that his mercurial performance of the previous weeks.

He doesn't care, she decided miserably. He really doesn't. Forget about his behaving like a jealous ex-lover; he doesn't even have a friend's concern for this situation.

Because of some unexpected scheduling changes, Friday was an exceptionally quiet day at Strictly Commercial. Except for two minor pieces of business that required her attention in the morning, Allie's calendar was completely open. She was saying as much to a pleasantly relaxed Donna shortly before noon when Chris walked into the reception area with a grim look on his face.

"Having a good time?" he inquired. September had brought a cool snap, and he was dressed for the weather in tan corduroys, a matching turtleneck pullover, and a zip-up jacket of buttery-soft brown suede. He perched himself on the edge of Donna's desk and fixed Allie with a cool stare.

She stared back, hating the way her pulse pounded whenever she saw or heard him. She'd hoped her physical reactions to Chris would ease over time, but that didn't seem to be happening. If anything, the reactions—and her aching frustration over them— seemed to be growing more and more intense.

"Donna and I were having a wonderful time," she said quietly. "It isn't often we get a day when we have five consecutive minutes of peace."

"Is that a complaint?"

"Just an observation."

"Ah." Chris glanced at Donna. "Well, I observe that there's nothing on the schedule for this afternoon, right?"

Donna made a show of consulting the main office calendar, the one with everybody's schedule penciled in on it. "You're all free as birds," she replied.

He nodded. "I suppose you're going to want to leave early for your big date tonight?" he said to Allie.

"Adam isn't picking me up until eight. I don't need a lot of time to get ready, so I was planning to stay here until my regular quitting time. Why?" She experienced a twinge of suspicion and—could it be?— hope. Was Chris suddenly going to come up with some last-minute work assignment that would prevent her from seeing Adam?

"What are you going to wear?" he asked abruptly, taking her completely by surprise. That was the last question she was expecting to hear from him at this point!

"What does that have to do with anything?"

"Just tell me."

"Why should I?" she countered.

"Why shouldn't you? Or aren't you planning to wear anything?"

"Allie, just tell him," Donna cajoled reasonably, trying to forestall a potentially explosive reaction to the last outrageous suggestion. The receptionist's expression held a degree of concern, but her eyes were bright with speculation.

Allie made a face. "I'm wearing my amber silk dress," she replied finally.

"Oh, the one you got on sale at Bloomingdale's last year?" Donna inquired with a diplomatic—if somewhat simulated—show of interest. She liked very trendy clothes and generally considered Allie's wardrobe too boringly classical for her taste.

Allie nodded confirmation.

"I like that dress," the receptionist declared. "It's . . . nice."

"Is *nice* all you're aspiring to tonight?" Chris made the word sound like an insult. Allie's back stiffened.

"What's wrong with nice?" she demanded. "And what's wrong with my amber silk?"

"Nothing's wrong with either one of those things, Allie. But there's nothing much *right* with them, either."

"I suppose you think I should parade around wearing something like that dress your date had halfway on last night?"

He looked blank for a moment. "You mean Marcia?"

Allie smiled sweetly. "She looks like she had a personal exemption from the law of gravity," she told him.

"Yes, well, she believes that if you've got it, you should flaunt it,"

Her chin went up. "And as we both know, I don't

'got it,'" she said flatly. "But what you've got, Chris, is a lot of nerve! Criticizing the way I do or don't dress—"

"Better me than Adam, don't you think?" he cut in bluntly. He glanced at Donna, who was taking in the exchange with rapt fascination. "Allie and I are going shopping," he informed her.

"We are not!" Allie protested instantly.

"Yes, we are," he corrected firmly. "This may take most of the afternoon, Donna. Hold the fort."

"Sure thing, Chris."

Allie gave Donna a look of wordless reproach before glaring at Chris again. "I am not going shopping with you," she muttered through gritted teeth.

"Honey," Donna announced as Chris silently picked up Allie's shoulderbag, took her arm, and began steering her inexorably toward the door, "you don't have any choice."

"Why are you doing this?" Allie asked for the fifth or sixth time as Chris shepherded her into yet another ultra-fashionable Manhattan boutique. This one featured oyster lacquered walls and an abundance of crystal and gilt. It looked like some expensive interior designer's vision of heaven.

"Perversity," he replied pungently.

"I don't need a new dress."

"That, Brown Eyes, is a matter of opinion."

"I don't *want* a new dress!"

"What you want—or don't want—and what you get aren't always the same thing."

The painful truth in that remark shut her up for a moment.

"Well, what about the green thing we saw in the place we were just in?" she asked in a restrained tone after a pause. "It was ni— attractive."

"It was nice. Period. We're looking for something special."

Special. Chris wanted her to look special for another man, for her ex-husband. Allie wanted to curl up and die.

A beautifully dressed, reed-slim saleswoman glided over. "May I help you?" she inquired, favoring Chris with a gleaming smile that held more than professional warmth. At least she didn't seem to know him. The women who had waited on them in three previous stores had greeted Chris by name.

Chris returned the woman's smile with lazy charm. "We're looking for something soft and sexy in a dress," he said. "Black would be best."

The words *soft* and *sexy* were beginning to get to Allie. "Maybe I should just wear my black lace slip," she suggested sweetly, her dark eyes mutinous.

"You can wear your black lace slip under the dress we're going to buy," Chris amended blandly.

The clerk ignored the exchange. "What size?" she asked, cocking her head slightly as she assessed Allie's tweed jumper and beige cowlnecked sweater. Allie had the distinct impression she wouldn't even rate a "nice" from the woman.

"Eight," Chris supplied.

"Mmm..." The woman pursed her well-glossed lips thoughtfully. "We've got a few things you might be interested in out on the rack already, but I think I've got just what you want in the stockroom. We received an exclusive shipment from one of our new designers this morning. Let me bring out a few dresses."

"Chris, I am not the type of woman who wears exclusive dresses from new designers," Allie said desperately after the woman moved away. "Tonight with Adam..." Her voice trailed off and she sighed, unable to put into words what she was feeling. Why couldn't Chris just understand?

He looked at her for a long moment, his green eyes enigmatic as he studied the distressed expression on her upturned face. When he finally spoke, it was in a low and carefully controlled voice.

"Allie, there are times when you have no idea what type of woman you are. Maybe tonight will help you find out. Now, let's go through the rack."

Allie obeyed him with a kind of stunned docility, unable to believe she had actually heard him right. She stood beside Chris, trembling inside, as he went through an elegant row of size-eight dresses with professional rapidity. He shook his head at garment after garment. Allie remained silent, the dresses passing in a blur before her indifferent eyes.

"Here we are," the saleswoman cooed several minutes later. She was carrying four basic-black dresses draped over one arm. She displayed them one at a time, providing a knowledgeable, soft-sell commentary. Two of the dresses were made of silk, one of embroidered lace and chiffon. The fourth was a simple sluice of fine wool jersey.

"Try that one on, Allie," Chris said after a moment of consideration. He nodded toward the fourth dress.

Allie, who had been fingering the cool, expensively sensual silk of one of the dresses with unthinking relish, looked at him in open surprise. Of the four offerings the woman had brought out, the wool jersey was by far the least glamorous. Indeed, it didn't seem to do much more than just hang limply in an unpromising fall of fabric. She thought the saleswoman looked a bit taken aback by his selection, too.

"Didn't you say something about soft and sexy?" she returned with a trace of challenge.

"Just try it on."

The dressing room the saleswoman showed her to was as elegantly appointed as the rest of the shop. Allie decisively declined the woman's polite offer of assistance; she had no desire to have her modest undergarments judged and found wanting on top of everything else.

Allie kicked off her shoes. She then stripped down quickly, pausing for a moment to assess her reflection. Shaking her head, she took the black dress from its padded hanger and pulled it on in one smooth movement. The waist was elasticized and tied with a narrow self-belt. After making a few adjustments and doing up the button at the neckline in back, Allie knotted the belt and then looked at her reflection.

She was surprised by what she saw. The soft matte black fabric flattered the creamy clarity of her skin and highlighted the soft sheen of her hair. The cut of the dress, which was simple to the point of severity, transformed her slenderness into a provocative asset. The slightly scooped neckline provided the perfect frame for her long neck and revealed the fragile lines of her collarbone. The subtle drape of the bodice and the slim skirt hinted at the body beneath with tantalizing style.

And the back! At first glance, it was just as chaste as the rest of the covered-up, long-sleeved garment. But there was a secret: it was slit from the single button at the neck to the waist, the fabric draped in such a way that only certain movements made this fact evident.

It was a sensual dress, not simply a sexy one. As oblivious as Allie had once been to such things, even she recognized the garment's impact as she stared at her reflection in the mirror. It was a dress a woman would choose to wear for herself . . . and her man.

And Chris had picked this as something she should

wear for *Adam*. He'd picked it as something with which to show her ex-husband that while she may not have been enough woman for him two years ago, she certainly was now.

Suddenly Allie was furious. Damn Chris! And damn herself for letting him do this to her! These past weeks she'd been blaming herself for whatever was wrong between them—blaming herself for falling in love, blaming herself for not being able to make him love her in return. Well, it wasn't all her fault, was it?

No!

She would have been able to go back to being his friend and colleague, she knew she would have! After all, she'd spent her whole life being one of the guys; and she would have been able to revert to that role with Chris, given the opportunity.

But he hadn't given her that opportunity, had he? His attitude toward her—for all his talk about working things through—had changed irrevocably once they'd gone to bed together. Oh, he might protest that their relationship was still special to him, but she realized now that what had happened in Antigua had made him take her out of the "friend" category and lump her with all the other women he'd made love to.

To hell with that! Allison Anne Douglas *was* special—to herself, if nobody else. Maybe she wasn't the perfect homemaker or the sexpot of the century, but if Chris was too blinded by male stupidity to see that, then it was his loss! And if he thought he could repackage her and pawn her off on her ex-husband, he had another think coming!

Yes, she was going out with Adam this evening. But because she wanted to! She'd knock his socks off! And she'd show Christian Cooper a thing or two at the same time.

Allie took off the black dress and put it back on

its hanger. After pulling her own clothes back on and giving her hair a quick swipe, she stalked out of the dressing room. She found Chris sitting on one of the rather spindly gilt chairs provided for waiting husbands, boyfriends, and shopping companions. He seemed totally unaware of the distinct interest with which he was being eyed by several of the shop's patrons. He rose lithely when he saw Allie, a faintly puzzled expression appearing on his face.

The saleswoman glided over, her skillfully made-up face wrinkling into a delicate show of concern. "Not what you were looking for?" she questioned.

"Actually, I wasn't looking for anything," Allie replied bluntly. "At least not when I came in here. But I'm going to take this dress."

"Ah." The woman smiled, obviously pleased by the sale but a trifle puzzled by Allie's statement. "Shall I ring it up?"

"Please. It'll be a charge."

"Thank you." Taking the garment, the woman moved off toward the register.

"I gather I'm not going to get a look at the dress on you?" Chris queried, his eyes narrowing as he searched Allie's face.

"You gather correctly. But don't worry, it doesn't remotely qualify for the adjective *nice*." She favored him with a pseudo-sweet smile.

"I didn't think it would with you in it," he countered, his tone as edged as hers. He glanced at his watch.

"Am I keeping you from something?" she asked.

"I told Parrish to expect us by five-thirty."

"Parrish?"

"Yeah. He's probably in your apartment now, setting up his gear." He gazed into her astonished eyes for a moment. "He's going to do your makeup for tonight," he explained simply.

It took Allie a few seconds to find her voice. There was nothing like having Chris's opinion of her inadequacies in the feminine wiles department shoved in her face!

She cleared her throat. "You're not taking any chances, are you?" she asked tautly, then walked off to sign for her new dress.

"Wait a minute," Allie said as the elevator door in her building slid open. Chris's palm, placed firmly in the small of her back, propelled her into the car. "You said Parrish is in my apartment?"

Chris pressed the appropriate button on the control panel. They'd made the cab ride from the clothing boutique in virtual silence. Allie's instinctive protest when he'd gotten out of the taxi after her, clearly intending to come inside the building, had died unspoken in her throat when she'd seen the determined, almost angry set of his features.

"That's right," he confirmed laconically, jamming his hands into the pockets of his suede jacket. He stared straight ahead as the elevator door whispered shut.

"And just how did he get there?" she demanded.

"With a key."

"*What* key?"

Chris turned his head to look at her. "Remember about a year ago when you went to Des Moines to see your father for Thanksgiving? You gave me the extra key to your apartment so I could water your plants. You never asked for it back. I lent it to Parrish."

"Oh."

They got off the elevator and walked down the hallway to her apartment. She had just started searching through her shoulderbag for her keys, when the door flew open.

"You're late," Parrish informed them.

"We're here now," Chris replied. He and Allie entered the apartment single file.

"I see you went to that new place on Madison," Parrish commented, nodding knowledgeably at the oyster-and-gold dress box Allie was holding. "And what did you buy?"

"*I* bought a basic black dress, Parrish," Allie answered, placing a faint but unmistakable stress on the pronoun.

The makeup artist's brows lifted and his snapping black eyes darted speculatively back and forth between Allie and Chris. "Ah, so it's like that, is it?" he drawled. "Well, never mind. You go take a shower or whatever, Allie. I'm ready for you anytime, and we don't have all night. I'm set up in your living room, darling. It's the only place with decent light." He shuddered. "Honestly, how do you put yourself together in the morning without decent light? By Braille?"

He sounded so disgusted, Allie couldn't help smiling. "I don't wear a lot of makeup, Parrish," she reminded him.

"Mmm, so I've noticed," Parrish said with delicate sarcasm.

Allie glanced from Parrish to Chris. "Well, I'd tell you two to make yourselves at home, but you've apparently already done that. I'll be back in a few minutes so you can finish up with your project of making a silk purse out of a sow's ear. Excuse me." And without giving either one of them an opportunity to speak, she turned on her heel and vanished into the bedroom.

After unfolding the black dress and hanging it up, Allie took off her clothes and donned her white cotton robe. She padded into the bathroom, where she found two sets of electric rollers placed pointedly on the counter next to the sink. Shaking her head a little, she dutifully plugged one set into the wall socket. Then peeling off her robe, she stepped into the shower.

Fifteen minutes later, her body fresh and sweet-smelling and her long thick hair neatly rolled up on the curlers, Allie returned to the living room.

"Okay," she announced with a trace of bravado in her voice and a very militant sparkle in her eyes. "I've just washed my face, Parrish. Let's see if you can do anything with it."

"Sweetie, you're going to be *surprised* at what I can do with it," Parrish replied, practically rubbing his clever, narrow-fingered hands together in eager anticipation. He slanted a look at Chris, who was sitting on Allie's couch, apparently engrossed in a local news program. "A lot of people are going to be surprised," he added. "But forget that for the moment. Sit down and let me take a really good look at you. I'm glad you took my little hint about the curlers."

"Little hint? I'll bet the entire nation of Guatemala doesn't have as many electric rollers as you left in my bathroom!" She sat down in the chair Parrish steered her to.

"That's why they call it an underdeveloped country," Parrish declared with an air of superiority. "Now, be quiet, please."

Although Allie disliked the notion of people fussing over her appearance—her occasional trips to the hairdresser for a trim and conditioning treatment left her itchy—she'd long been fascinated by the skill and perfectionist's devotion Parrish brought to his work. Having him suddenly focus his professional attention on her was disconcerting. Having him do so in front of Chris was just plain disturbing; it lent an intimacy to the situation that Allie found totally unsettling.

A woman needs a few secrets, she thought, fighting to surpress the memory of how little about her Chris— her confidant and friend of two years and her lover of four days—didn't know.

Did he know she loved him?

"Allie! Will you stop scrunching up your face?" Parrish commanded in an outraged tone. "My God, it's like trying to paint the Mona Lisa on a prune in the middle of an earthquake!"

"Sorry," she apologized, wondering if Chris found Parrish's outburst funny. Before Antigua, they'd often laughed together about his antics. But now...

"You should be sorry. I canceled a booking to do this because Chris insisted it was— *Now* what's wrong?"

Allie blinked. "Nothing. Your hands are cold."

Parrish made a disbelieving sound. "That wasn't my hands. It was a sponge. Just hold still, darling, please?"

He worked deftly, muttering to himself from time to time. With her thoughts in a whirl, Allie barely registered a quarter of what he was saying, but she did glean enough to discover that Parrish liked the unplucked line of her eyebrows, deplored the fact that she hadn't thought to dye her long, light-brown lashes, and positively couldn't fathom her failure to realize what an absolutely wonderful jawline she possessed.

"What are you doing now?" she asked curiously as he feathered a light brushstroke around her forehead.

"Highlighting," he explained succinctly. "The product's called Gilding the Lily. Close your eyes."

She obeyed and heard him picking through his extensive collection of sable brushes. She felt a delicate dabbing at the outer corner of her lids. "More highlighting?" Parrish had already used at least a dozen different products on her eyes.

"Uh-huh. Open your eyes and look up. You need another coat of mascara."

"Another one?"

"Yes. And for heaven's sake, take it off with oil when you clean your face. Don't use that atrocious soap I saw sitting in the bathroom! If you've been washing your face with that, Allie Douglas, it's a wonder you haven't turned yourself into a wrinkled crone. You'd be better off using scouring powder and steel wool on your complexion. Will you please look *up?!"* There was a brief, breath-holding silence. *"Voila!"* he announced.

"Are you finished?"

Parrish was studying her critically. "For the moment. Chris? What do you think?"

Green eyes searched Allie's face silently. The artificial color Parrish had so delicately applied to her cheeks deepened.

"I think she should get dressed and do something with her hair."

Surprisingly, the makeup artist took this evasion in stride. It was Allie who felt a stab of hurt lance through her.

"That's a good idea," she said tersely, getting up. Parrish hadn't provided her with a mirror, so she was more than a little anxious to know what she looked like. "Thank you, Parrish," she said, dropping a light kiss on his café-au-lait cheek.

"Thank me when you're completely put together. Oh, here"—he handed her a silver tube of lipstick—"you'll need this for a touch-up. And *please,* don't smear everything when you put on your dress! I don't have time for a major repair job."

One look in the full-length mirror on the back of her bedroom door told Allie that Parrish's nagging complaints about her failure to live up to her potential had been stunningly on target. The makeup artist hadn't tried to transform her into something she wasn't; he'd simply made the best of what she was—and could be. He'd balanced the angularity and strength of her features by emphasizing her expressive brown eyes and the vulnerable curve of her mouth. Suddenly her face belonged to a woman who was confident and comfortable with men, but emphatically *not* one of the guys.

Allie dressed quickly, feeling both eager and apprehensive. After pulling the electric rollers out of her hair, she brushed it out and then coiled the honey-brown tumble into a loose, stylish knot at the nape of her neck. A few rebellious tendrils floated free despite a misting of hair spray, but she left them untamed.

She thrust her feet into a pair of black sandals and clipped on a pair of gold knot earrings. After a light whoosh of perfume and one final glance in the mirror, she was ready.

But ready for what, she wasn't certain.

Taking a deep breath and squaring her shoulders, she returned to the living room.

Chris was helping Parrish pack up his gear. The makeup man was in the middle of stuffing a handful of sponges into his custom-made burgundy snakeskin case when Allie walked in.

"Far be it from *me* to try to offer *you* advice about women, Chris," he was saying in an intense undertone. "But what you're doing— *Allie!*" He nearly slammed the lid of the case on Chris's hand. A proud smile creased his face.

"Well?" she asked. Not quite ready to meet Chris's eyes, she concentrated on Parrish's reaction.

"Not *well,* darling: terrific!" It was a crow of triumph.

"Thank you." Tilting her chin in an unconscious gesture, she glanced over at Chris. The look he gave her was so complex, so . . . scalding, it made her breath stop at the top of her throat. But before she could even attempt to decipher the turbulent emotions she saw, a shuttered expression came down over his face, locking him in as uncompromisingly as it shut her out. The rejection couldn't have been any clearer if he'd hit her.

Allie started breathing again. "What do you say, Chris?" she asked quietly. "Do you think Adam will approve?"

"What man wouldn't?" Although he spoke quietly, there was something savage in the way he pronounced the words.

"Look, dear hearts," Parrish cut in, scooping up his equipment. "I hate to break this up, but it *is* almost eight o'clock." He headed toward the door. "And, besides, I've got a hot date. Coming, Chris?"

"I'll be there in a minute." Chris's eyes hadn't moved from Allie's face.

"I'll count the seconds," Parrish declared, opening the door. "Before I go, I've got just two things to say: Allie, you look beautiful; and Chris, you're a damned fool."

He left, allowing the door to slam shut behind him.

Allie moistened her lips daintily with her tongue. She knew Parrish well enough to realize that his parting shot had been prompted by something a lot more genuine than his penchant for theatricality. But what the something was . . .

"You're not going to wear that tonight are you?" Chris asked sharply.

"That" was the gold-and-coral bracelet.

Allie twisted the bangle around her wrist. "You don't think I should?"

"No."

"All right." She took it off. Then, goaded by something she couldn't explain, she asked, "Do you want it back?"

"No!" For a moment, the shuttered expression cracked open. Then he was back in control of himself again. "Just don't wear it tonight, please."

She set the bracelet down with unsteady fingers. "I think you'd better go now," she said. "It's almost eight. Adam will—"

"—be here soon. Yes, I know. Don't worry. I won't ruin it for you."

"Ruin?" What on earth did he mean by that?

Before she had a chance to ask, he'd crossed to her and cupped her chin, very gently, in one hand. "Parrish was right, you know," he said softly. "You are beautiful, and I am a damned fool. Adam Phipps is a lucky man, Brown Eyes."

And with that, he bent his head and kissed her tenderly.

He walked out the door without saying good-bye.

Chapter

9

ALLIE LEFT FOR dinner with her ex-husband, the feel of Chris's kiss still tingling on her lips. The caress had not been long or deep; indeed, he had done little but claim her mouth for a few heady seconds before releasing her and walking out. Yet the kiss had burned like a brand and ignited a firestorm of questions.

Adam took her to The Four Seasons. Allie knew he had picked the famed restaurant to impress her, and she was flattered. During most of their marriage, he had never actively sought her goodwill, although he had devoted a great deal of energy to trying to impress his co-workers, his superiors, and his friends. Even when things were right between them, it never would have occurred to Adam to wine and dine her; Allie simply hadn't inspired that kind of treatment.

She had been to The Four Seasons once before, with Chris. The occasion was a luncheon with a client and several ad agency account executives. It had been May then, and the restaurant's décor—along with the staff's crisp uniforms, the table appointments, and the lavish menu—had reflected the delicate freshness of spring.

All that had been altered with the changing of the seasons. The place now exuded a bold, autumnal mood. The menu, with its distinctive mix of American and international dishes, reflected the flavors of fall and the spirit of a good harvest.

The food was superb. Adam dined on iced oysters with hot *chipolata* sausages—an unlikely-sounding but delicious combination—and roast quail with sage and fried grapes. Allie ordered a cream of vegetable soup followed by broiled lamb chops. The service was attentive without being oppressive.

Allie enjoyed herself . . . to a point. The setting was elegant and the company pleasant, even charming. But it all seemed so pointless, so empty.

Why, oh why, had Chris kissed her like that?

"You really have changed," Adam observed quietly as they lingered over their coffee.

Allie's mouth curved into a rueful little smile. "Are you saying that because of the way I look tonight?" she asked. Adam's reaction when he'd first seen her that evening had been all she could have wanted, and more. If she'd had any doubts at all about the impact of her new makeup and dress, his stunned expression and momentary speechlessness had dispelled them.

"That has something to do with it," he conceded honestly. "I mean, Allison, you're a knockout. I never really realized . . ." He paused for a moment, frowning into his coffee cup. "Then again, maybe I never really looked."

"There wasn't all that much to look at," Allie said lightly.

He gazed across the table at her. "I'm serious," he said. "You *have* changed. You've got so much more confidence, so much more . . . I'm not certain how to put it into words, but I can feel it." He hesitated visibly for several seconds. "I've changed, too," he began slowly. "At least I like to think I have. I blamed you for so many things—"

"Adam," she interrupted. "Please, don't. That's in the past."

"But it was my fault. I had such a narrow-minded view of what a good wife was supposed to be and I tried to force you—"

"What happened between us wasn't a matter of your fault or my fault. We both made mistakes. I wasn't what you wanted. I should have known that."

"I hurt you."

"Yes," she admitted. "But I lived through it, Adam."

"I wish I could make it up to you."

"There's nothing to make up."

They left the restaurant and walked for a few blocks in the crisp night air, talking of this and that. Finally Adam flagged down a cruising cab. He gave the driver Allie's address before settling back beside her.

"Would you like to come in for a nightcap?" Allie asked when they arrived at her building.

Adam smiled at her. "Yes, I'd like that very much."

He said some pleasant things about her apartment after they were inside, and even recognized the over-stuffed chair from their place in Chicago. Allie accepted his compliments with a smile, knowing that her decorating skills were still as haphazard as they'd been during their marriage.

She poured two brandies, breathing a silent prayer

of thanks to the distillery-owning client who had demonstrated his appreciation of Strictly Commercial with a generous and very costly assortment of liqueurs. Chris had divvied up the gift among the staff.

"Mmm." Adam inhaled the heady aroma of the brandy before taking a sip. He was sitting in the middle of the sofa. After a moment's pause, Allie sat down about a foot away from him.

She knew he was going to kiss her even before he put his brandy snifter down on the coffee table with a decisive clink. She knew, and in a strange way, she welcomed it. She even kissed him back a little.

The search of his mouth over hers was pleasant enough. His lips were warm and familiar, and stirred up a few enjoyable memories, but that was all. The devastating, devouring explosion of passion Chris's kisses had evoked in her was simply not there. Allie didn't think it ever had been.

Adam broke the kiss first, lifting his lips from hers with a sigh of frustration. He edged back and picked up his brandy glass. He swirled the amber liquid around in the snifter for several seconds before speaking.

"You're in love with somebody, aren't you?" he asked.

Allie could feel her heart thudding painfully within her breast. There was no accusation or lurid curiosity in Adam's question, only a sort of regretful resignation. She nodded once, very slowly.

"Chris Cooper?"

She took a shaky breath and exhaled it. Averting her eyes, she twisted a tendril of hair around one finger. "Yes," she confirmed in a quiet voice. It was the first time she'd admitted it aloud to anybody—including herself.

"Then why did you go out with me tonight?"

"Because I wanted to."

"But didn't he—"

"As far as Chris is concerned, he and I are friends. Colleagues. He has no idea how I feel about him. Or if he does"—she waved her hand—"it doesn't matter."

"I don't believe he thinks of you only as a friend. The other day at your office, during the meeting—"

Allie shook her head fiercely. "Chris was the one who picked out this dress I'm wearing," she said. "And he arranged for somebody to make up my face." She gave a humorless little chuckle. "If I have changed, he's the reason. He's the one who should be taking bows for the way I look tonight."

Skepticism was plain on her ex-husband's handsome face. "Allison, if that's true—"

"It is."

"Then, I'm sorry."

She shrugged, fingering the soft fabric of her dress for a few seconds as she stared down into her lap. Finally, she looked up at him again. "Don't be sorry, Adam. It's just one of those things. I'm all right, really."

They chatted almost impersonally for a few more minutes, and then Adam rose to leave. Allie walked him to the door, feeling as though a chapter of her life was being finally and irrevocably closed. As disjointed as some of this evening had been, she realized it had helped her resolve a great many emotions about the past.

"Well, I guess this is good-bye ... in a way," Adam said. "We'll probably be seeing each other professionally—"

"It will be fine," she told him quickly, not wanting to share her fear that the professional side of her life might be falling apart along with the personal one. "Let's say good night and not good-bye."

"Okay." He nodded and touched her cheek lightly. "Chris Cooper is a lucky man," he said quietly. "But he's even stupider than I was if he doesn't realize what he's got in you."

Allie wandered disconsolately around her apartment, clearing away the brandy bottle and snifters and tidying up a bit. She had no conception of the passing time; everything seemed curiously suspended.

Sighing, she ran through the messages that had accumulated on her answering machine. There were the usual irritating hang-ups, an ego-boosting comment from Parrish, a call from her brother Rick, and one from her father. Idly, she flicked the switch that kept the recording part of the machine on but allowed her to monitor the calls as they came in. Sighing again, she padded into her bedroom where she undressed and brushed out her hair. Then she went into the bathroom. After cleansing her face—with oil, as Parrish had ordered—she decided to take a bath.

It was around half-past midnight when the call came in. With her mind drifting and her eyes closed in an effort to ease the tension that had been building within her all evening, Allie barely registered the sound of her own voice:

"Hi! Congratulations! You have reached the answering machine of Allison Anne Douglas and you now have the once-in-a-lifetime chance to win a return phone call from her. All you have to do is answer these three questions correctly after the sound of the beep. One: what is your name? Two: what is your phone number? And three: what do you want? Good luck! And here's the beep!"

What she heard next was so unexpected, she didn't quite believe it at first.

"Hi, Allie, this is Chris. Damn . . . I really hate

these machines—even yours. Look, we need to talk. Call me, will you? Please."

Allie stared at the tile walls for several seconds, the beating of her heart thudding heavily in her ears. Slowly, she began rinsing off her body. Then she rose carefully and stepped out of the tub.

After toweling off, she wrapped herself in her white cotton robe and went into the living room. She studied the answering machine for a few moments, regarding the device as though it was an enemy. Frowning, she pressed the button that rewound the tape. She spun back through Chris's message, then played it again just to be sure.

She stood there, breathing in and out, in and out. She and Chris needed to do more than talk, but she wasn't certain she could handle it. Not tonight. Still . . .

Her lips tightening with decision, Allie crossed to the phone. She punched out Chris's home number from memory. There was a little click on the line as the connection went through, and then the disheartening sound of a busy signal.

Allie hung up and dialed again, thinking she might have made a mistake. The busy signal sounded again. She dropped the phone back into its cradle.

Suddenly feeling very weary, Allie moved to the couch and sat down. Who could Chris be on the phone with at this time of night? If he needed to talk with her, why hadn't he left his line free?

She curled her legs up under her, stifling a yawn. She'd give it fifteen minutes and try again.

Her head started to droop. She blinked once or twice, her eyelids growing leaden. Why had Chris called?

Fifteen minutes . . .

She dozed off without realizing it. Fifteen minutes became thirty. Forty. An hour.

She woke up with a start, stiff-necked and disoriented, a few moments before three. She rubbed her fingers against her temples. The throbbing she had been aware of earlier was still there, heavier and more draining than before.

The phone and the answering machine were silent.

Allie got up, hugging herself. Three in the morning. If Chris had really needed—wanted—to talk with her, he would have called back before this, wouldn't he? She nodded to herself, making up her mind.

She'd phone him in the morning.

Allie slept much later than usual the next day, not waking until nearly ten. When she finally got out of bed, her first move was to go to the telephone and call Chris. The events of the previous day pressed down on her with an unforgiving weight.

She let the phone ring until the hollow, electronic sound became a mockery.

She tried once more about an hour later, just before she went out on her usual round of Saturday errands. Still no answer. There was no answer for the rest of the weekend.

Her own phone rang only once during that time. Allie was out when the call came, and whoever it was hung up without leaving a message.

Monday morning was spent obtaining permits for a location shoot in Central Park. While this was a job Allie could have done over the phone, she decided to take care of it in person. She told herself that it would actually be easier that way, but in truth, she was none too anxious to get to the office and see Chris.

After her appointment, she caught a cab headed uptown, but quickly realized that the late Monday morning traffic was slower and more snarled than usual. After about fifteen minutes of jerky, stop-start progress, she told the driver to pull over and let her out. It was only a dozen or so blocks to the Strictly Commercial studio, and she didn't mind the exercise.

Allie liked autumn. In her mind, it was the season that suited Manhattan best. The crisp, cool weather seemed to enliven everyone, bringing a fresh new rhythm to the city. Street performers—some of them spirited amateurs just showing off, some budding professionals trying to earn a little money—blossomed at unexpected intervals along the sidewalk.

The heels of Allie's boots clicked on the pavement as she walked along. She tried not to think about Friday's confusing turn of events. Her hands were stuffed into the pockets of her slightly oversized blazer, the jacket layered over a white silk shirt and an argyle knit vest. She'd tucked her customary jeans into the tops of her boots, and her braided hair swung jauntily back and forth as she moved.

She arrived at Strictly Commercial shortly before noon. Donna greeted her with an expression of gratitude and a stack of phone messages.

"Thanks, Donna," Allie said, wondering at the receptionist's unusually harried manner. She shuffled quickly through the slips of paper, then tucked them into the outer pocket of her shoulder tote. "How was your weekend?" she asked.

"Not half as interesting as yours, I'll bet."

"What?" Allie's heart skipped a beat and her voice was a few notes higher than normal.

Donna eyed her curiously. "How did your date with your ex-husband go?" she inquired.

"Oh, that." Allie felt strangely relieved. "It was . . . nice. He took me to The Four Seasons."

The receptionist gave a long, admiring whistle.

"Honey, I'd be satisfied if my boyfriend took me to *one* season!"

Allie laughed briefly at the joke, then grew serious. She nibbled at her upper lip for a moment before speaking. "Is Chris around?" she asked, irritated by the tentativeness of her tone. She was going to have to sort things out with him sooner or later; putting it off wasn't going to provide any magic cure.

Donna grimaced. "Unfortunately, yes."

"Unfortunately? What's wrong?"

The receptionist sighed heavily. "I've been wondering that ever since you two came back from Antigua," she declared bluntly. "But all I can say at the moment is that Chris is in the worst mood I've ever *seen*. I'm going to post a quarantine sign or put up storm warnings or something. He definitely—but definitely—got up on the wrong side of the bed this morning."

"And what side of the bed did you get up on today, Allie?" Chris's voice interrupted coolly. He sauntered into the reception area like a predatory jungle cat: lithe, lazily graceful, yet unmistakably dangerous.

"Uh-oh," Donna said softly. She hunched down into her seat as though trying to make herself as inconspicuous a target as possible. "Big trouble," she added under her breath.

Allie felt the same way, with much more reason.

"Hello, Chris," she said, a prickle of alarm running through her. He was spoiling for a fight; that much was plain. But why? Why the anger? And why the innuendo-laden question?

He ignored her greeting. "Maybe I should ask *whose* bed you got out of," he went on, moving to within a foot of her.

She stiffened. "What's that supposed to mean?" she challanged.

His mouth curved into an unpleasant smile. "I take it your dinner with Adam turned into a full-scale reconciliation," he drawled. His green eyes raked over her. There was a harshness to the set of his features that she had never seen before.

Allie clenched and unclenched her hands. "Isn't that what you wanted?" she retorted acidly, telling herself it didn't matter what he thought. After all, he was the one who had practically pitchforked her into Adam's arms! Except for that one moment of farewell at the door...

"You spent the weekend with him."

"What if I did?" She raised her brows in an effort to communicate what she hoped was indifferent superiority. "I really don't think it's any of your business. Especially not at this point." Tossing her head, she turned on her heel.

Chris grabbed her and spun her back to face him. "The hell it's not my business," he ground out from between gritted teeth.

"The hell it is!" she spat back, temper flaring in her wide brown eyes. She tried, unwisely, to pull herself free of him. "Let go of my arm," she ordered.

He responded by tightening his grip. "Not until I get an answer to my question."

Allie's brain was shrieking a warning to be careful; she ignored it, plunging heedlessly along the path dictated by hurt, angry instinct.

"Forget it, Chris," she said, trying to jerk away again. "You've got no right—"

"Damn it, I've got every right! If I'm going to lose you to that—"

"*Lose me?*" she exploded, too caught up in her own stormy emotions to see the sudden desperation in his eyes. "Don't flatter yourself! You never had me!"

He flinched, then shook his head very slowly, very deliberately. She could see a vein throbbing in his temple and sense his barely leashed fury. For a moment, she was genuinely afraid. Once he started to speak again, the fear was overwhelmed by a blinding sense of outrage.

"Oh, I had you, Allie," he said in a soft, lethally seductive voice, his words insultingly intimate. "I had you in just about every way a man can have a—"

She slapped him. It was no ladylike smack of protest, either; this was a blow that carried the full force of her arm behind it. The sound of her palm meeting his cheek held a sickening violence.

There was a shocked silence. Allie was too appalled to speak. She felt very close to being physically ill in reaction to what she had done.

Chris released her, lifting his hand to rub the side of his face. The reddened imprint of her slender fingers was clear against his tanned skin. He drew a shuddery breath, then exhaled it sharply.

"Hitting me isn't going to change things between us, Allie," he said in a flat, ruthlessly unemotional voice.

She gave a bitter laugh. It was either that or cry, and she had too much pride to break down in front of him. "Things between us changed when I went to bed with you in Antigua," she told him. *And when I woke up the next morning and realized I was in love with you,* she added silently. "You'll never know how sorry I am for that."

She blinked, fighting back the tears. Chris said nothing.

"Look," she went on after a moment. "I've got three weeks of vacation coming to me. I'm going to take some of that time starting now. If you don't like it—well, maybe it would be better all around if you just fired me. Maybe it would have been better all around if you'd never even hired me."

Donna said something as she walked out the door, but Allie didn't check her pace; she just kept on going.

Chris didn't say anything. He didn't try to stop her.

Allie walked home in a numbed, blank-faced state. She arrived at her apartment too exhausted to do anything but slump down onto her couch and cry. She sobbed silently for a long, long time, weeping in anger and hurt and grief.

The sense of inadequacy that had left her so vulnerable in her marriage to Adam reasserted itself with cruel force in those first few hours.

Oh, yes, you had me, Chris, she thought miserably, rocking back and forth. But it wasn't enough, was it? I couldn't give you what you want from a woman... I can't even give you what you need from a friend anymore.

She cried herself out eventually and sat there drained and empty, staring at her walls. From time to time she sniffed or bit her lip. She wiped at her cheeks with the back of one hand in a childlike gesture.

She barely reacted when someone knocked imperiously on her door. "Go away," she whispered.

There was another knock. "Allie? It's Parrish! Open up."

Parrish. What was he doing here?

"Allie! Unless you want me to do something really embarrassing, open the door."

She did. Parrish bustled in carrying a large shopping bag. Once inside, he put it down and surveyed her with the air of a man who has seen everything.

"You," he announced, taking in her pale face, swollen eyes, and red nose, "look absolutely terrible. What is it? Some kind of allergic reaction?"

The angelic innocence in his voice as he asked the question alerted Allie to the fact that he was probably very much aware, in detail, of what was wrong.

"Oh, Parrish," she said, shaking her head.

"Well, cheer up, sweetie. At least you don't have a black eye."

She gasped. "I didn't give Chris a black— Parrish!"

He shrugged. "A slight exaggeration. Donna says he *is* sporting a slightly fatter lip than usual on his big mouth. Really, darling, I had no idea you were so . . . primitive! I mean, honestly, if I'd known, I never would have thrown myself at that handy-dandy tennis pro the other week in an effort to save your virtue. I would have let you belt him one in the chops."

He was being deliberately, distractingly outrageous, and Allie was grateful for it. For all his faults and foibles, Parrish made it impossible for a person to wallow in self-pity. She gave a crooked smile.

"That's better," he approved.

"Why are you here?" she asked. "I take it you've been talking to Donna."

"Ah, yes. I've had a firsthand report from the war zone. As to why I'm here: well, *somebody* had to make certain you hadn't done something stupid."

Her chin came up. "You don't have to worry about that."

The bright bitchiness in his expression faded, leaving him looking serious and a bit sad. "But I do, Allie," he said simply. "I always worry about my friends doing something stupid." His voice sharpened again. "And, if I may say so, judging by what's been going on between you and Chris recently, I've been right to worry!"

Allie sighed. "I appreciate your concern, Parrish, but there's really nothing you can do at this point.

There's nothing anybody can do."

He folded his arms over his chest. "You know, for a little while there, I thought you two were finally coming to your senses. I was hoping that Antigua would make you realize . . . I mean, after nearly eighteen months of my nudging you at each other, it finally looked as if something was going to happen."

Oh, something had happened all right!

"You've been *nudging* us?"

"Somebody had to do it! Do you have any idea how frustrating this buddy-buddy routine of yours has been? Two people who are obviously made for each other, and all you want to do is be *friends*. God, I could just scream! And now this—this . . . whatever it is going on between you. I'm ready to wash my hands of the whole situation, Allie. Really, I am." He made a huffy sound of disgust.

Allie stared at him in stunned disbelief. "You think that Chris and I—"

"I think, Donna thinks, Martine Lurie thinks," he announced flatly. *"Everybody* thinks. Except you two. But I don't think you've been thinking at all. Now, that's all I'm going to say. I brought you a bag of goodies. I find pigging out helps in times of emotional crisis. And don't tell me you're not hungry, darling, or I'll really get worried about you."

There was a long pause. "Parrish," Allie said slowly, "what am I going to do?"

"Anything but what you've been doing."

Allie tried to keep herself busy over the next two days, but images of Chris—each one more vivid than the one before—kept threatening to upset her painfully maintained equilibrium. Her body as well as her heart ached, and she felt increasingly restless and uncertain.

Parrish's words, especially his blunt parting shot, echoed in her brain at odd, unguarded moments. Part of her wanted to act on those words, to seek Chris out and talk, really talk; but part of her was still desperately afraid and angry. She had once thought she understood Chris as well as she understood herself, yet the events of the past month had transformed him into a virtual stranger and started her wondering about who and what *she* was, as well.

She still loved him; that remained unchanged. She realized, looking back over the past two years, that she had probably been in love with him for a long, long time.

A Wednesday night phone call from her father added one more unsettling variable to her situation.

"I'm taking a few days off," she explained, replying to her father's affectionate inquiry about how she was doing.

"I didn't know you had any vacation time scheduled. Last time we talked, you said you were awfully busy."

"Oh, well, things change. It just seemed like a good time to get away."

"Any chance of getting away to Des Moines?"

"I'd probably better stick around the city, Pop."

"You think things might change again?"

Allie, who was curled up in the overstuffed chair in her living room, chewed on the tip of one slender finger. "Something like that," she agreed. For the first time in a long while, she wished her mother was still alive. Although she and her father were extremely close, there were a few things she couldn't talk to him about simply because he was her father—and a man.

"J.J. mentioned you'd seen Adam again." It was a probe; an unusually delicate and discreet one by Douglas family standards, but a probe nonetheless.

"Adam's the new head of the advertising department at FideliCo. Strictly Commercial does their TV work. He was in New York on business. That's how we saw each other."

"Hmm." He sounded dubious.

"We went out to dinner one night."

"Did you have a nice time?"

Allie closed her eyes at the word *nice*.

"Allie?"

"Yes, Pop, we had a nice time. We're both different people than we were when we were married." She gave a self-conscious little laugh. "I think I like him better now that I did two years ago. But there's no chance of our reconciling. In fact—"

"I see. And how's Chris?"

Out of the frying pan, into the fire.

"Oh, he was in rare form last time I saw him," she answered with perfect honesty, then gnawed on her finger again. "Pop," she said slowly, "did you and Mom fight much? I mean, when you were married?"

He chuckled as though savoring a memory. "We had some real doozies, your mother and I," he said. "She had quite a temper. Fiesty—that's what she was. You got that from her, Allie. And, of course, your big brown eyes."

"Cow's eyes, according to Rick."

"Rick always did enjoy deviling you. Not that you were any angel, young lady. Just the other day, I was up in the attic going through a few of J.J.'s things and I ran across something that reminded me of the time when—"

"Pop, when Mom and you used to fight, how did you make it up?" she broke in. "Didn't you ever say or do awful things? Unforgivable things?"

"Allie, Allie, unless you're so pigheaded you're going to nurse a grudge for the rest of your life, nothing's unforgivable. And believe me, a grudge makes pretty poor company when the nights get long and cold. Now, I'm not going to stick my nose into your private life—J.J.'s always saying that I keep forgetting you're twenty-seven, not seven—but whatever it is that's making you ask these questions, I just want to remind you that once you get through forgiving somebody for the supposedly unforgivable things they've said or done, you get to make up with them. That tends to take the sting out of the fighting."

"Oh, Pop, I love you," Allie said softly.

"I love you, too, sweetheart."

Allie thought about what her father had said all that night and most of the next day. She realized that while she still didn't understand what had made Chris act the way he had, she'd already forgiven him. She loved him, even though she remained achingly uncertain of his feelings for her. And it was that uncertainty that held her captive, made her fearful of taking the first step back toward him.

Parrish seemed to think that Chris felt as strongly about her as she felt about him. At least Chris had admitted to feeling *something;* if he hadn't, they never would have become lovers and could have gone blithely on with their uncomplicated friendship. Yet, if he felt anything more that a physical yen for her, why hadn't he said so?

Why had he ended their affair after four days and started dating every attractive woman in sight? Why had he given her the bracelet? Why had he reacted so uncharacteristically to the situation with the tennis champion?

And why, why, *why* had he all but served her up to Adam on a platter?

More to the point: why hadn't she had the courage to challenge him on any of it?

Finally, late Thursday afternoon, Allie reached for the phone and dialed Chris's number at Strictly Commercial. Donna answered.

"Hello," the receptionist said. "Hello? This is Strictly Commercial. May I help you?"

Allie's throat had gone completely dry.

"I know somebody's there. I can hear you breathing."

"Donna?" she finally forced out.

"Allie? Is that you? Where are you? Are you all right?" The questions came out rapid-fire, like machine-gun bullets.

"Yes, it's me. I'm at my apartment and I'm fine. Is Chris there?"

"Oh, honey, no, he isn't. He had that location shoot out on Long Island today. At least I think it was Long Island. This place has turned into chaos central since you . . . went on vacation. When are you coming back?"

"I'm not sure I am. That's something I have to talk to Chris about."

"You're working up to a face-to-face, huh?"

"Well . . ."

"I understand. Look, he'll probably be back in the city before long. They had to cut things short because of the rain."

"Rain?" Allie had been so caught up in her own thoughts, she hadn't even bothered to look out the window.

"Uh-huh. It was only drizzling this morning, so they took a chance and went out. I guess they got about halfway through when the sky opened up. It's still pouring out."

"I hadn't realized. Uh, Donna, if Chris comes back, will you tell him— No, will you call me?"

"Sure thing. You know, you might try his apartment in a little while. He didn't say he was coming back here for certain. He didn't say much when he called about the shoot, as a matter of fact."

Suddenly, the bell on Allie's apartment door shrilled. She stiffened at the unexpected sound.

"Allie?" Donna asked curiously.

"Somebody's at my door," Allie said. "I've got to go. Thanks, Donna."

The receptionist gave a deprecating laugh. "No need to thank me. This is purely self-interest. The sooner you and Chris get things straightened out, the easier my life is going to be. Hope to see you soon. *Very* soon."

"Bye, Donna."

Allie's apartment building was somewhat lacking in security features, and although the door sported the latest in locks, it lacked a peephole.

"Who is it?" she asked, her hand hovering on the deadbolt.

"It's Chris, Allie."

"Chris?" She whispered his name, wondering if she'd suddenly started hallucinating.

"Allie, open up, please. We have to talk. I need a friend, Brown Eyes, and you're the best one I've got."

Chapter

10

"WHAT HAPPENED TO YOU?" Allie blurted out, genuinely shocked by the sight that greeted her when she finally opened the door. She was too shaken up to take refuge behind clever or casual comments.

Chris's dark curly hair was plastered wetly to his skull. His battered track shoes squished soddenly as he stepped inside her apartment. His ancient tan Burberry raincoat was drenched, dripping all over her floor.

She didn't care if he flooded out the entire apartment.

"I had to park about ten blocks away, and I didn't have a damned umbrella," he answered flatly.

"But you look *terrible*." She was appalled to see how tense and tired he appeared. He seemed pounds thinner than she remembered, and there was a disturbing, unfamiliar tension in his lean features. Her first, powerful instinct was to reach out and touch . . . soothe . . . love.

He managed a crooked grin that tore at her heart. "You don't look so hot yourself," he replied, coming very close to the old teasing tone he had used with her so often in the past. But there was nothing remotely teasing in the hungry expression in his eyes.

Allie felt herself flushing. She averted her gaze for a moment, suddenly aware of her bare feet, patched jeans, and faded University of Illinois sweat shirt. Her hair—at least it was freshly washed!—was carelessly pulled back into a ponytail, and her face was totally devoid of cosmetics. If Chris resembled a half-drowned dog at the moment, she probably looked like something a very undiscriminating cat would drag in.

"I wasn't expecting anybody," she mumbled. "Come in . . . if you want to. I'll take your raincoat."

"Toss it in your bathtub," he advised, slipping out of the soggy garment and handing it to her.

She nodded. "Right. I'll get you a towel . . . or something."

Great, really great, Allie, she scolded herself as she practically scurried off. Chris is here—he came to you—and you start off by telling him he looks terrible and proceed onward to playing the proper little hostess.

Well, what was she supposed to do?

Talk. He'd said they had to talk; he'd said that in the message he'd left on her answering machine, too, the night he'd sent her off with Adam.

He'd said he needed a *friend.*

"You can dry off with this," she announced, returning to the living room with one of her bath towels. Chris was sitting on the couch. He'd removed his shoes. The bottoms of his jeans were wet, as was the upper half of his navy turtleneck.

He took the fluffy white towel wordlessly and rubbed his hair with it, blotting up the worst of the moisture. She could not help but notice the smooth play of muscles revealed by the close-fitting knit shirt.

"Do you want something to drink?" she asked, clearing her throat and shifting her weight awkwardly. She didn't know what to do with her eyes ... her hands ... her body. "Coffee? Brandy? Brandy's good if you've had a chill. Or—"

"Allie, please, don't," he said softly, cutting off her nervous chatter. "Don't be like that with me, not now." He slung the towel around his neck.

She chewed the inside of her lip. "How do you want me to be with you?" she asked tautly. "The way I used to be?"

Pain flared deep in his green eyes. "We both know that's impossible, don't we?"

Oh, Lord! Blindly, she found her way to the opposite end of the couch. Now she understood why he had come.

What he said next took her totally by surprise. "This towel smells like you, you know."

"What?"

He sniffed one corner of the towel. "It's got your scent: sweet, natural ... sexy." His voice dropped a note.

She stared at him blankly. I've gone crazy, she decided, unable—unwilling—to credit what she thought she was hearing.

"You know, that first day you walked into Strictly Commercial about the job, you were like a breath of clean, fresh air. I could've gotten high on just being near you. Until I saw what was on your face."

"My face?"

He reached out, very slowly, and stroked one finger lightly down her cheek, then withdrew his hand as if he didn't trust himself to touch her further. The controlled tenderness in the contact made her tremble.

"You had your chin stuck out the way you do when you're scared or angry or just being spunky," he recalled quietly. "It was almost like you were daring life to take a swing at you. But one look in your eyes and I knew that something—or somebody—had already swung and hit. Swung and hit and *hurt*. All I wanted to do was take the hurt away . . . and keep it away." He stood up, turning from her. "But I seemed to have screwed that up pretty well, haven't I?" he asked bitterly.

Allie shook her head in instant denial, her mind flooding with memories. Impelled by an instinct she couldn't name, she got up, too, and moved to him. His entire body stiffened at her approach.

"You did take away the hurt, Chris," she whispered. "You were . . . you *are* my friend. And I'm yours."

He turned around so quickly, his eyes dangerous with such intense emotion, that she took an involuntary step backward.

"That's not enough!" The words sounded as though they were being ripped out of him. "Don't you see? I'm in love with you."

"You're in love with me?" She could feel the blood draining from her face. She swayed a little.

He caught her by the shoulders, steadying her— and himself.

"You never said anything," she protested in a tiny voice. At this moment, her only link with reality was the possessive grip of his palms.

"I didn't know what to say. All my life, until you, *love* was either a word you said to get what you wanted, or a word somebody used right before they stuck a knife in your heart. The way I felt, the way I feel about you . . . Oh, hell, Allie, I was scared! I'm still scared."

"But why?" Why was he frightened of loving her?

"Because I'm not in charge anymore. Because somewhere along the line, you've become such a part of me." His hands on her shoulders tightened almost to the point of bruising before he released her. "You know, I love you so much I thought I was going to be able to stand by and let you go back to your ex-husband, but I can't. I know it's what you want, but I can't."

The meaning of his words hit her like a bolt of lightning, illuminating his actions of the past weeks with mind-boggling clarity. The hope she had refused to feel at his first confession of love exploded within her.

"What I want?" she questioned. "Are you crazy?"

There was nothing remotely restrained about the tone she used; it was vintage Allison Anne Douglas and she saw, from the sudden, flickering change in his eyes, that he recognized it.

"Out in the Hamptons, you said you still had feelings for him. And your face when you saw him—"

"I was married to Adam for five years! Of course I still have feelings for him. I can't just rip out a piece of my life, Chris. But whatever I feel for him, it certainly has nothing to do with wanting him back. And as for my face . . . Lord, I was surprised, that's all."

His dark brows came together and he focused on her with a tangible intensity. Just as she had fought against hope a few minutes before, she sensed he was doing the same thing now.

"Then why did you go out to dinner with him?"

She threw up her hands. "Because I was curious. Because I was flattered that somebody wanted me; you certainly didn't seem to once we got back from Antigua! And because I was jealous. I mean, you seemed to be competing for Bachelor of the Year honors or something—" Her voice broke and she whirled away from him.

She knew how close he was even before his hands closed around her upper arms with cherishing tenderness. His palms were warm and gentle even through the fabric of her sweat shirt, but they were no more steady than her voice had been.

"That night I came over to watch bad movies with you, you said Adam's name as I was carrying you to bed," he recalled softly.

She flushed. She still had no rational explanation for that, except that she had been half asleep and deeply confused by everything that had been happening to her. She had known in her heart that it was Chris, even as her slumber-fogged brain was producing Adam's name.

"You were the one I asked to stay," she said fiercely. She felt the pressure of his hands forcing her to turn around. After a moment's instinctive resistance, she gave in. Her chin came up slowly and she met his eyes. "I wouldn't have done that if I still wanted Adam, if I still loved him. I wouldn't have done that any more than I would have gone to bed with you in Antigua if I hadn't . . . hadn't . . ."

"Wanted me?"

"Loved you!" she burst out. "I love you, all right? I don't know how or when . . . I don't even really know *why*, considering the treatment I've been getting."

He kissed her then, devouring her mouth with the hunger of a starving man, yet savoring the delicate flesh with the finesse of a connoisseur. Her lips parted on a moan of pleasure. She felt the slick sweep of his tongue over hers. The taste and heat of him invaded her.

His hands stroked down her back until his palms were cupping the curves of her buttocks. He drew her closer, then closer still, fitting her to him. Her pelvis rocked in a languid, unmistakably erotic rhythm, responding to the driving need she felt erupting within him.

Her strong, slender arms swept up and she locked her hands around his neck, fingers laced through the springy curls of thick dark hair at the nape. She shuddered in a starburst of pleasure as he took her tongue into his mouth with a sweet, tantalizing suction.

He nipped teasingly at the full lower curve of her lip, then kissed each corner of her mouth as though staking his claim on it. His eyes were brilliant. The weariness she had seen in him earlier had vanished like fog before the warmth of the sun. The tension was still there in his features, but it was a tension of straining eagerness, not anxiety or unhappiness.

Bewitched by the look and feel of him, Allie tracked the strongly marked line of his dark brows with one finger. She traced the shape of one of his eyes, feeling the fine skin of his lids and the lush thickness of his lashes. She learned the proud strength of his nose and the carved sensuality of his mouth. His tongue flicked out to taste the tip of her wandering finger.

"Did that give you any clue as to *why?*" he asked huskily.

"It's not just sex—" she began.

He silenced her with a quick, hard kiss. "I know that," he answered, punctuating his words by touching her eyelids and the tip of her nose with his mouth. "Why do you think I've been acting like what Parrish so succinctly called 'a damned fool' all this time? Sex

I could handle, Brown Eyes. But love . . ."

She melted against him, feeling the beat of his heart against her cheek. Her old inhibitions, her old insecurities, were gone. "Love *I* can handle," she murmured. "It's the sex part I've never been too certain about."

"Be certain about it."

"But, Chris!" She let out the giddy exclamation as he swung her up into his arms. "What are you—"

"Last time I was here, you told me I could stay and I said I couldn't. If the invitation still stands, I want to change my mind. I'd like to stay forever."

She answered with a brief but glorious smile, then pulled his head back down for a kiss. Her eyes fluttered shut.

Her body was yearning for him, aching for his possession, by the time they reached her room. But instead of laying her down on the bed as she expected, he placed her gently on her feet. Opening her eyes, she saw from his expression that his desire was as urgent as hers; she also saw his determination not to rush this moment.

She gave him another smile, this one wise and womanly. Sliding her palms up his broad chest, she relished the faint roughness of the knit of his turtleneck and the deepening rise and fall of his breathing. He was right: this was a time to savor and cherish.

His hands moved from their resting place on her hips to her waist and then slipped under her sweat shirt. His fingers explored the naked, silken skin of her torso with passionate appreciation, eventually trailing upward to seek and claim her breasts.

How perfectly they fit his hands! She had no need for reassurance, but if she had, the message was there in the passionate adoration of his touch.

She could feel her nipples stiffen to eager buds

under his sensual persuasion, and she gave a shaky little sigh. "Oh, Chris..."

"How beautiful you are," he murmured, bending to kiss her. She parted her lips, inviting, inciting, a deepening of the caress.

When he finally released her, it was only to tug her sweat shirt up and over her head, leaving her bared to the waist. He stripped off his sweater a moment later. Reaching around behind her head, he snapped the elastic band that had been holding her hair back off her face. His fingers tangled briefly in the tumble of honey-brown, then danced over the quivering skin of her shoulders.

"You make me beautiful," she said, warming in the heat of his tender scrutiny. She reached out for him with her open arms... and her open heart.

They made love. Created it. Celebrated it. The time-honored rituals, the most ancient of rhythms, became new. It was an ecstatic voyage of discovery that was tempered with a sense of homecoming.

She was a temptress, and he was her willing victim. He was a sorcerer, and she was his eager apprentice. They were two people who had let down their defenses, not surrendering to each other but embracing what they were together.

Gentle, teasing touches turned to more demanding caresses, and tantalizing whispers gave way to inarticulate groans. The tender wooing of gliding fingers and licking tongues became the elemental explosion of merging flesh.

They loved.

Afterward, they lay next to each other, their bodies intimately tangled. There was a silence of exhilaration and exhaustion, and a sublime feeling of completion.

"Were you really jealous after we came back from Antigua?" he asked her softly, toying with her hair.

It was not a smug question; instead, she heard a kind of wondering satisfaction in it. She lifted her head a little so she could look at him.

"Yes," she answered simply. "I kept comparing myself with all those other women you were—you were—you know . . ."

He put a finger to her lips. "Compared with you, Allie, there are no other women." He smiled with a trace of rueful self-mockery. "And you can spare yourself the search for a euphemism for what I was supposedly doing with all the others. I was trying to keep my mind—to say nothing of my hands—off you. It didn't work."

"No?" Secure in his arms, she actually felt able to tease him. "What about the soap opera queen?"

"Oh, her."

"Yes, her."

"At the risk of seeming ungallant, let's just say that I'm probably the first man who ever took her out for the evening and left her on the doorstep with a handshake instead of a kiss."

Allie smiled, then dipped her head and very daintily flicked her tongue over one of his nipples. He made a throaty sound as she teased the stiff nubbin of flesh, then nuzzled her cheek pleasurably against his chest, enjoying the crispness of his dark mat of chest hair.

"You know, turnabout's fair play," she observed slowly.

"If you're leading up to asking if I was jealous of your ex-husband, the answer is yes."

"And yet you dressed me up for him?"

"I told you. I thought you wanted him. And I wanted to make you happy."

Her eyes were radiant with tenderness. "You're amazing."

"According to Parrish, I'm crazy—or at least I

was until about an hour ago. I think even he'll admit that I've finally come to my senses."

"We've come to *our* senses," she corrected. Her expression grew thoughtful. "Last Monday, when we quarrelled... What you thought about Adam and me—"

"I was half out of my mind, Allie. God, I'd been driving myself crazy over you since we got back from Antigua. I still wanted you so badly, but I couldn't reconcile that with the idea of needing you as my friend. Anyway, when you didn't call me back after I left the message on your machine, something snapped. All I could think of was you and Adam."

"But I did try to call you back, Chris. Your line was busy."

He groaned. "Parrish. He phoned to read me the riot act on how I was throwing away the best relationship I was ever going to have with a woman. He had a lot to say on the subject." He paused. "I guess what really made me flip out was when I called again Saturday and got your answering machine. I couldn't leave a message. Pride, I guess. Or pigheadedness."

"Were you too pigheaded to pick up the phone when it rang?" she asked, remembering the pain of listening to his phone ring and ring and ring.

"You tried to reach me Saturday?"

"And Sunday. There was never any answer."

He sighed. "When I didn't hear from you Friday night, I jumped to a lot of conclusions about you and Adam and decided I had to get away. So I went out to the Hamptons."

"Oh, Chris."

He heard the regret in her voice. "It's over, Brown Eyes. Let's not dwell on the past, okay? Except maybe to learn from it. And even then, I'd much rather enjoy the present. Mmm..."

"Hmm-mmm?"

"And talk about the future."

Allie stilled. "The future?"

He nodded, running one finger down her left arm. Once he reached her hand, he lifted it and pressed it to his lips. "Where's your bracelet?" he asked.

"I took it off when I showered," she said, mystified by the change of subject. "But, Chris?"

He got out of the bed, tall, lean, and utterly superb in his male nudity. She held her breath without realizing it as he moved lithely across the floor, then disappeared into the bathroom. He returned a few seconds later and sat down on the edge of the mattress. Taking tender possession of her left hand again, he slipped on the beautifully crafted gold circlet with ritualistic care.

"I never really answered your question about why I gave this to you," he said quietly, fingering the piece of jewelry. He slid it around and around her wrist for several seconds. "I suppose that was because I hadn't figured out the reasons myself. Or maybe I had, and I wasn't ready to admit them."

"Chris . . ."

He enclosed her hands with his own and took a deep breath, silencing her protest with a shake of his head. His steady, passionately serious gaze held her motionless.

"Look, you've been special to me in a way no other woman has ever been. Since the first day you walked into my life. I know you have this hang-up about not being attractive to men but, believe me, I was attracted to you from the very start. But my usual instincts got sidetracked by a need—a desire—to protect you. So we became friends. And that was a first for me. For a while, I was able to tell myself that our friendship was the key to your specialness. But the problem was: the closer we got, the stronger the attraction grew. I wanted you so much I ached with it. Finally—"

"Antigua," Allie whispered. She knew how hard it was for Chris to make this confession to her. It was, in a sense, the ultimate affirmation of his love: the baring of his heart.

"Antigua," he affirmed. "I think I must have been out of my mind that first morning. I watched you sleep for about an hour, feeling like I'd just made love for the first time in my life. In a way, I had; but at that point I didn't understand the difference between having sex and making love. Anyway, I was happy, sad, proud, and absolutely terrified. So, naturally, I ended up behaving like an idiot." He cupped her face in his palms. "What you said to me that first morning, about going back to the way things used to be—you thought that was what I wanted to hear, didn't you?"

Allie nodded. "I was scared, too, Chris. That first morning, that was when I realized I loved you. But you had always been so down on the idea of a long-term relationship with a woman, and then you started talking about working things through."

"I behaved like an idiot," he repeated. "As for your bracelet: I wanted to give you something special, but I didn't know how to tell you that. I wanted to put my mark on you somehow, but I also wanted to deny there were any strings attached. All I can say in my own defense is that I had a lot of lessons to unlearn. And even though it's taken me a while, I think I've finally done it. I know how to tell you I love you now, Allie. I love you as a friend and a lover. And I don't want to deny the strings or the attachments anymore. In fact..." He hesitated, the expression in his green eyes commandingly male yet deeply vulnerable. "In fact, I read somewhere that when a man gives a woman a bracelet, he's really preparing her hand to wear his ring."

It took her a second to comprehend the meaning of his last words. What he had said before had made her heart soar with joy; she could scarcely believe she could reach a higher plane of happiness.

"Are you asking me to marry you?"

He nodded. "You see," he went on carefully, "it's a cinch we can't go back to being just buddies. And I think Antigua proved an affair isn't going to work, either. So, since our professional relationship has always been . . . ah, Strictly Commercial, I think our personal relationship is going to have to be strictly matrimonial."

"Does it matter what *I* think?" she asked, a sparkle of mischief lurking behind the suddenly luminous beauty of her face.

"It always matters what you think," he replied, easing her gently back down on the bed. His face was vivid with tender laughter.

"In that case, I think you're absolutely right!"

When ecstatic sensation finally gave way to the first languid reassertions of rationality, Allie stirred voluptuously in Chris's arms.

"Parrish is going to be very pleased once he knows," she observed drolly, planting a kiss on Chris's chin. His skin tasted faintly of salt and its texture was slightly roughened by the shadowing of new whisker growth.

"He probably knows already. In fact, he's probably taking credit for getting us together."

"He *did* mention something about nudging us."

"Do you think your family will be pleased?"

Allie thought she heard a tiny and endearing trace of anxiety in the question.

"Are you kidding? Pop and my three brothers are going to be happier than Parrish."

"Really?"

"Really. You've already been given the Douglas stamp of approval. Now, I don't pretend to understand why, but it apparently has something to do with your being the type of man who would beat somebody up on my behalf."

"Ah." It was a sound of pure masculine satisfaction.

"That makes sense to you?"

"Naturally."

She made a little face. "Maybe I'm not as much one of the guys as I thought."

"One of a kind, Brown Eyes, yes. One of the guys—no way. You're all woman, Allie: strong, sensitive, and sexy. And I love you."

"I love you."

They smiled into each other's eyes, making silent vows that the happiness and security of this moment would be preserved for the future.

"It's funny how things work out," Chris mused, fondling her breast with gentle, arousing fingers. "We started out friends at first—"

"—and ended up lovers at last," Allie completed.

Chris sighed. "Until I met you, Allie, I always thought men and women had to be one or the other with each other."

She laughed softly. "Stick with me," she teased. "You'll be surprised what you'll learn."

He joined in her laughter. "As I've said many times before, I don't know what I'd do without you."

Allie stretched languidly. "Rest assured," she told him, "you'll never have to find out."

Second Chance at Love.

___ 0-515-08204-X	FOR LOVE OR MONEY #230 Dana Daniels	$1.95
___ 0-515-08205-8	KISS ME ONCE AGAIN #231 Claudia Bishop	$1.95
___ 0-515-08206-6	HEARTS AT RISK #232 Liz Grady	$1.95
___ 0-515-08207-4	SEAFLAME #233 Sarah Crewe	$1.95
___ 0-515-08208-2	SWEET DECEPTION #234 Diana Mars	$1.95
___ 0-515-08209-0	IT HAD TO BE YOU #235 Claudia Bishop	$1.95
___ 0-515-08210-4	STARS IN HER EYES #236 Judith Yates	$1.95
___ 0-515-08211-2	THIS SIDE OF PARADISE #237 Cinda Richards	$1.95
___ 0-425-07765-9	KNIGHT OF PASSION #238 Linda Barlow	$1.95
___ 0-425-07766-7	MYSTERIOUS EAST #239 Frances Davies	$1.95
___ 0-425-07767-5	BED OF ROSES #240 Jean Fauré	$1.95
___ 0-425-07768-3	BRIDGE OF DREAMS #241 Helen Carter	$1.95
___ 0-425-07769-1	FIRE BIRD #242 Jean Barrett	$1.95
___ 0-425-07770-5	DEAR ADAM #243 Jasmine Craig	$1.95
___ 0-425-07771-3	NOTORIOUS #244 Karen Keast	$2.25
___ 0-425-07772-1	UNDER HIS SPELL #245 Lee Williams	$2.25
___ 0-425-07773-X	INTRUDER'S KISS #246 Carole Buck	$2.25
___ 0-425-07774-8	LADY BE GOOD #247 Elissa Curry	$2.25
___ 0-425-07775-6	A CLASH OF WILLS #248 Lauren Fox	$2.25
___ 0-425-07776-4	SWEPT AWAY #249 Jacqueline Topaz	$2.25
___ 0-425-07975-9	PAGAN HEART #250 Francine Rivers	$2.25
___ 0-425-07976-7	WORDS OF ENDEARMENT #251 Helen Carter	$2.25
___ 0-425-07977-5	BRIEF ENCOUNTER #252 Aimée Duvall	$2.25
___ 0-425-07978-3	FOREVER EDEN #253 Christa Merlin	$2.25
___ 0-425-07979-1	STARDUST MELODY #254 Mary Haskell	$2.25
___ 0-425-07980-5	HEAVEN TO KISS #255 Charlotte Hines	$2.25
___ 0-425-08014-5	AIN'T MISBEHAVING #256 Jeanne Grant	$2.25
___ 0-425-08015-3	PROMISE ME RAINBOWS #257 Joan Lancaster	$2.25
___ 0-425-08016-1	RITES OF PASSION #258 Jacqueline Topaz	$2.25
___ 0-425-08017-X	ONE IN A MILLION #259 Lee Williams	$2.25
___ 0-425-08018-8	HEART OF GOLD #260 Liz Grady	$2.25
___ 0-425-08019-6	AT LONG LAST LOVE #261 Carole Buck	$2.25

Prices may be slightly higher in Canada.

Available at your local bookstore or return this form to:

SECOND CHANCE AT LOVE
Book Mailing Service
P.O. Box 690, Rockville Centre, NY 11571

Please send me the titles checked above. I enclose _____ Include 75¢ for postage and handling if one book is ordered; 25¢ per book for two or more not to exceed $1.75. California, Illinois, New York and Tennessee residents please add sales tax.

NAME_____

ADDRESS_____

CITY_____STATE/ZIP_____

(allow six weeks for delivery)   SK-41b

QUESTIONNAIRE

1. How do you rate _____
   (please print TITLE)
   ☐ excellent   ☐ good
   ☐ very good   ☐ fair   ☐ poor

2. How likely are you to purchase another book
   in this series?
   ☐ definitely would purchase
   ☐ probably would purchase
   ☐ probably would not purchase
   ☐ definitely would not purchase

3. How likely are you to purchase another book by
   this author?
   ☐ definitely would purchase
   ☐ probably would purchase
   ☐ probably would not purchase
   ☐ definitely would not purchase

4. How does this book compare to books in other
   contemporary romance lines?
   ☐ much better
   ☐ better
   ☐ about the same
   ☐ not as good
   ☐ definitely not as good

5. Why did you buy this book? (Check as many as apply)
   ☐ I have read other
     SECOND CHANCE AT LOVE romances
   ☐ friend's recommendation
   ☐ bookseller's recommendation
   ☐ art on the front cover
   ☐ description of the plot on the back cover
   ☐ book review I read
   ☐ other _____
     _____
     _____

(Continued...)

6. Please list your three favorite contemporary romance lines.
   _____
   _____

7. Please list your favorite authors of contemporary romance lines.
   _____
   _____
   _____
   _____
   _____
   _____

8. How many SECOND CHANCE AT LOVE romances have you read? _____

9. How many series romances like SECOND CHANCE AT LOVE do you <u>read</u> each month? _____

10. How many series romances like SECOND CHANCE AT LOVE do you <u>buy</u> each month? _____

11. Mind telling your age?
    ☐ under 18
    ☐ 18 to 30
    ☐ 31 to 45
    ☐ over 45

☐ Please check if you'd like to receive our <u>free</u> SECOND CHANCE AT LOVE Newsletter.

We hope you'll share your other ideas about romances with us on an additional sheet and attach it securely to this questionnaire.

• •

Fill in your name and address below:
Name _____
Street Address _____
City _____ State _____ Zip _____

Please return this questionnaire to:
   SECOND CHANCE AT LOVE
   The Berkley Publishing Group
   200 Madison Avenue, New York, New York 10016